Vicki Hendricks lives in Hollywood, Florida. She teaches English and creative writing at a local college and has recently become an avid skydiver, which started as research for a forthcoming novel.

For Elisa Albo and Kyra Belán,
My remarkable poet and artist friends
Who have inspired and energized me
Throughout the torturous process of creating

iguana love

••••••••••••••••••••

vicki hendricks

Library of Congress Catalog Card Number: 98–89868

A catalogue record for this book is available from the
British Library on request

First published 1999 by
Serpent's Tail,
4 Blackstock Mews, London N4 9NT

Website: www.serpentstail.com

Phototypeset by Intype London Ltd
Printed in Great Britain by Mackays of Chatham, plc

10 9 8 7 6 5 4 3 2 1

Acknowledgements

Much gratitude to my agent Elizabeth Ziemska for her intelligent perseverence in getting my work to the right people. Also thanks to Shane O'Neill, Dick Lanam, Michael Pontecorvo, and David Owen, for advice on navigation and devices.

Power is the ultimate aphrodisiac.
Henry Kissinger

1

◆◆◆◆◆◆◆◆◆◆◆◆◆◆◆◆◆

The dark side of my mind took control on one of those slippery-hot Miami nights about a year ago, the start of my unraveling, my spin into psychosis and murder.

That night I began to picture myself alone, Ramona Romano, free, without Gary – a simple thought. I paced in front of the windows and stared out between the frosted jalousies in the door, as usual, wrapped myself in the feel of moonlight on water, imagining the beach a short distance away, smelling the salt. We had no air and it was hot and still. I was hot – in all parts of my body. Gary read the paper and watched TV, but I couldn't settle down. No cuddling next to him – like in the old days when my head was full of wedding pictures and other people's smiles. His kisses had begun to sting. They were like free-floating jellyfish cells in the ocean. Not searing pain, but constant annoying itches. I had pity for him but no love.

I stripped and sat there in bra and panties under the ceiling fan next to Snickers, my rex cat. With short, curly hair, she was a perfect adapter to the tropics same as I, but she could stretch out and relax, whereas I couldn't settle down. My system was electric, pores shooting sparks, teeth hurting to bite, nails aching to claw. I felt pressure rattling my lungs, like I couldn't get a decent breath. Life was all around, but I wasn't supposed to have any.

I saw my past as a chain of mistakes caused by weakness and vulnerability. I'd married young, not knowing myself, taking my mother's goals, and keeping the name she'd given me. I had no ideas of my own. All the planning and gifts, the dresses and flowers gave me something to think about instead of the promise "forever." I'd done what I should in my mother's opinion, going to nursing school for a career, finding a hardworking husband without tattoos. Gary never laid a patch of rubber when he took off up the street, never said *fuck* within my mother's range of hearing.

But caring for others didn't fulfill me like I expected, and neither did Gary's lovemaking. His lean, muscled body and thick blond hair couldn't save me from my chosen trap, a prison of guilt. I hated Gary's love for its restrictions. I didn't yet realize that being the object of love is the highest source of power.

Gary and I had spent our first few years together in Lansing, Michigan, our hometown. But I always dreamed of living in the tropics, near the ocean. I finally convinced him we should move to Miami, to put fresh feeling into our marriage, leave the cold, conservative Michigan "deathstyle" for the freedom of a warm climate. I made it sound good. I could find a nursing job anywhere, and he could start his own landscaping company, great business all year round.

We packed up a U-haul and left the slush and soot and hard-work ethics. Florida meant freedom from cold and boredom and normal life. We set ourselves up in an apartment with a pool, only a few miles from the beach – close enough, I thought, for my dreams. I found a nursing job and Gary started cutting lawns, trying to get some yearly contracts.

He talked about home, but I never did. I dug that sand. I was born again in Miami, into a style that fit, my own religion, my own species. I was reptilian, my blood heating in sync with the tropics. Fuck if I could stop it. Fuck if I wanted to. That night I couldn't sit there another minute.

"Gary?" I called from the bathroom to the living room where he was watching TV. I put toothpaste on the brush. "I'm taking your truck, going out for a little while."

"Where?" he called back. "Mona, where are you going?"

By then I was scrubbing my teeth, making garbled sounds in answer, like I was under water – where I wanted to be. I spit and rinsed and dashed into the living room to get the keys from the hook.

"I'll go with you," he said.

I walked past. "I'm going down to the bay. Just for a look at the water."

I went back, plunked my ass on his lap, and took a kiss, sucked at his lower lip. I was back up before he could get his arms around me. I patted his tousled head. "Just wait till I get home, hon."

He reached to tweak my thigh under the shorts and let his hand drop. "Be careful," he said.

I tried to walk out instead of fly. Relief was a rush when the door closed behind me.

I knew a bar near Biscayne Bay – Seabirds – where the divers hung out. I'd met several of the guys at the shop where I'd recently been certified. It was my first time at Seabirds, but in seconds I knew I belonged. The discussion was on spearfishing as I scooted my stool up to the bar, but I could feel the pulse of sex under the surface of their conversation, inside the taut nylon of their Speedos. I felt the easy flow of sex in the tropics. Its tangy scent was heavy in the salty humidity drifting off the ocean.

That night I had a fling – one wild night would be enough, I thought. It was safe sex – no expectations – but it was hot, scorching with freedom. Waves of pleasure dragged me farther from Gary, way out beyond the safe waters of our marriage.

He must have known. I came home after four, high and cocky with myself, sweaty, but he didn't ask questions. I worked him hard from on top and his face relaxed into its bleary, peaceful look, now that I was back with him. I figured he was trying to let me get through what I needed, instead of starting trouble. But I couldn't control my appetites. I wanted to fill myself with the sensual mystery of the divers and their ocean – forever.

From then on, all I thought about was getting out for a dive. My dreams, day and night, took on one color, the sparkling blue of open water. But the boat ride and the rental scuba gear were expensive. Gary and I argued. He said diving was a luxury that had to wait. I could go for a dive for my birthday present or Christmas – months away.

I tried for weeks to soothe my cravings, stay home, watch TV, fulfill my chosen obligations. I tried not to think. I floated through hours of Cousteau documentaries, languishing in his French accent, swaying to the rhythm of waving sea fans, straining for a long look at gobies that disappeared into their holes, and searching for flounder eyes in the sand. I was obsessed. I wanted to eat a fish live, like Jacques Cousteau, when he surfaced on the mini-sub, plucked a bittersweet orange wriggler from the indentation of the hatch, and cupped it into his mouth. I tasted its slickness on my tongue and felt the crunch of tiny bones.

My world was focused within the limited peripheral vision of a dive mask. Instead of calming my lust, the sea nourished the fantasies that took me away from Gary.

Soon I was there again – twice a week, at Seabirds. I'd caught myself on fire, and I thought I could find someone to put it out. And yes, more than once I left with a man, fucked him, went home and tried to make it all up, do the impossible.

One night a diver brought a photo of his girlfriend in snorkel gear being towed on a line behind a boat. She was holding onto a life preserver – scanning the bottom for lobster, he said. The picture was taken in the Keys, in a few feet of water, and plush turtle grass shone like filaments under the surface. Half a body-length behind her was a dark gray shadow, a flat torpedo silhouette over two times her length, three times her width. The shark never attacked. No one even spotted it until the picture was developed, but the diver identified it as a tiger shark, a type known for aggression.

I was fascinated by that image – that startling, unhealthy balance. I didn't understand the dynamics, her power over him, but the two were beautiful together. I held that picture close to my chest and studied it in the smoky bar light. I saw freedom to dare and a challenge to brute strength by her innocent power. It started a tingling in my stomach and a flooding of blood

into my face, an adrenaline rush. I was going to be there no
matter what.

2

◆◆◆◆◆◆◆◆◆◆◆◆◆◆◆◆◆

Once the affairs got started, it was impossible to hang on to a household routine. I tried to pull back, but already I was a different person. I remember one evening, Gary doing the dishes, gently wiping each plate with the sponge and following my face with his eyes. He'd suddenly started helping out with the chores. He knew what was going on. I didn't try to be sneaky.

I put wet glasses into the cabinet and threw dripping silverware into the drawer, in a hurry to do my duty and escape that long-lashed smothering look of devotion. He dragged his forearm across the counter, pushing the pots into the sink with a bang and splashing soapy water on the floor.

"Jesus Christ!" he yelled. He stood staring at me like I was a kid. "Why do you think we have towels?"

I turned my head away from his red pumping face. I knew it was my fault.

"Look at me. You're always somewhere else. Let me look at your fucking beautiful face if I want to. You're my goddamn wife."

"What?" I said. I was caught with a look I couldn't control. He knew he was right.

"I'm sorry!" I yelled. "Sorry, Gary." I felt his pain in my chest. It made me wild with anger at myself. I pulled him to me and grabbed his hair in the back and clutched his head to my shoulder until I could get his tongue in my mouth and drag him into the bedroom.

I squatted over him in my raging guilt, while he slid into me hard with grief. I moved up and down, coming in waves and surges, until he finished. He reached to find the sweat puddled in the small of my back, the sign to him that he could still do it for me. He had passion confused with love – an easy mistake.

A few nights later we decided to splurge on dinner at a fancy Thai restaurant. It was Gary's idea for another start. I wanted it to work as much as I knew it couldn't. The phone rang as we stepped outside, and Gary went back to answer it. I could tell there was trouble the way he motioned to me with the receiver.

It was Enzo, a diver and captain for the dive shop, wanting to meet me at Seabirds. We'd traded innuendoes one night until he'd had to leave. Enzo, a dark circling shadow in my mind, cool, mysterious, always in control, outside reality. Enzo. Long dark lashes and curly hair. I pictured him at the helm, cocky and relaxed, yet sculptured in stone. Even his name made me ooze. He must have gotten my number from the shop files. He wouldn't know that I was married – who would, the way I acted? I doubted he would care.

I didn't lie. I told Gary it was one of my diver friends down at Seabirds. I tried to make it light. The words put him over the edge. His driving became erratic. He screeched to a stop at a red light.

"You're not going anywhere without me," he roared.

His volume fueled me, but I spoke calmly. "I told him you and I were just headed out." The words were true, but I didn't mention my plan to meet Enzo later.

The light changed and somebody beeped. Gary looked straight ahead and pressed the gas. "Okay." He took a breath. "We're going to have a good time."

I looked at his large tousled profile against the sunset. I never understood Gary's love or his pain. Newspaper and TV sports had taken up all his spare time until I'd been with other men. After that he spent hours caressing my body, every inch, and listening to my fantasies, all too late. We talked about a trip

someday – Australia – kangaroos and koalas in the Outback, the
Great Barrier Reef. He planned to sign up for diving certification
as soon as we had the money. By then it was the last thing I
wanted, but I helped him soothe his wounds, kept thinking I could
change.

That night at the restaurant he started on whiskey and soda.
He was half sloshed before we got the main course. I watched
him and made a design of linked circles with the base of my water
goblet on the glass tabletop – the Olympics logo gone wild. He
stared at me with watery eyes. I knew everything was my fault,
but my stomach was grinding and my blood crackling as usual.
He kept up the talk, but I could only manage to nod at his plans
for us and eat my shrimp curry.

When we got home, he turned on the TV and I went into the
bathroom to pee and brush my teeth. I needed out of there. I was
weak and immature, drawn to the lures of freedom and adventure,
as if I could handle them. My mother's voice was in my head, a
lurking conscience, but it didn't slow me down. I called Enzo's
mobile from the bedroom and agreed to meet him in half an hour.
I strode through the living room without stopping for a kiss. Gary
looked up from the TV as I hit the door.

3

◆◆◆◆◆◆◆◆◆◆◆◆◆◆◆◆

I got to Seabirds around eleven. It was a dim, shadowy, rough-wooded place with portholes for windows. Fish nets strung with lobster balls and twinkling Christmas lights stretched across the ceiling. Dried blowfish hung in the corners, looking cheerful with their tiny plastic eyes and pursed lips. At the bar, oysters on the half-shell were heaped on ice and I smelled the tang of the ocean coming off them.

The lounge was about two-thirds full when I walked in, but I didn't see Enzo, and it had been forty-five minutes. I felt heat rising in my chest. I had a feeling he wasn't going to show.

I looked around and recognized another diving instructor at the far end of the bar – Charlie. He was a couple inches shorter than I was, and probably ten years older, thin and sinewy as a Cousteau. He had sun-bleached blond hair and a leathery tan.

I'd never spoken to him, except once at the shop when he was working, but I'd watched him at the bar. He would sit on a stool at the edge of conversation, listening and smirking, keeping his stories to himself, while Enzo entertained with his adventures in Japan, his dives for abalone and coral.

I walked toward the rear. There was some mystery in his light blue eyes – I thought I might explore. He worked in the dive shop and taught with Enzo. I walked toward the vacant seat next to him.

I felt the men's looks as I walked the length of the bar. I had
on a T-shirt and shorts, a slice of each cheek sticking out. My red
hair in a ponytail bobbed with the feel of a buoy in the waves.

Charlie's head didn't turn. He had his chin in his palm and
was frowning toward the cigarette in his other hand. I stood next
to him and leaned over his shoulder to get his attention. I pointed
at the cigarette. "Bad example for your students."

His eyes rolled up toward me. Then he looked around. "None
of my students here," he said. His eyes went back to the cigarette.

I checked to see if Enzo had come in. No sign of him. It was
irritating. I put my hand on Charlie's shoulder. He was cold stone.
I didn't mind. Any place seemed better than home.

"What about embolism?" I asked. "Smoking and diving?"

He glanced back, took a long drag, and blew the smoke out
the opposite side of his mouth. "So you're my doctor, or what?"

"I could be your nurse."

He adjusted his jaw. "Oh, yeah, you're a nurse."

He stubbed the cigarette out. It was down to the filter. I took
another look toward the front for Enzo. I sat down.

His eyes stayed on the ashtray. "I'm cutting down."

The bartender came over and I ordered a draft.

Charlie gave a half smile. "Diving's been great," he said, "forty
to fifty foot visibility. Haven't seen you on the boat for a while."

"It's expensive – the fee and equipment rental. I can barely
afford a dive a month."

"I'm just saying you might want to get yourself in gear – mini-
season is coming up."

"Don't worry. My ass is always in gear," I said. "Nothing I'd
rather do than go down for the first lobsters." The beer was taking
hold and I was noticing how nice and compact he was on the
stool next to me. His legs were blond, tan, and lean in comfortable
fitting blue shorts.

I took a glance around. Still no Enzo.

He looked at his watch. The diver's swivel made it seem huge
and heavy on his thin wrist. "I'll let you finish your beer in peace."

"Oh," I said. "You're leaving me to the sharks?"

"I think you can handle them," he said.

I cocked my head. "By the way, have you seen Enzo tonight?"

"You mean, speaking of sharks?" He shrugged. "I don't keep track of Enzo's schedule."

I tried a laugh. "You saying Enzo bites?"

Charlie lowered his eyes and shook his head. He had something to say, but decided against it. "We're not really friends. We just work together," he said. He looked straight into my eyes for the first time, then looked back down. "Enzo has money, you know – all the women are after him."

I frowned. "I don't know anything about that."

"Good way to keep it."

He slid from the stool and walked off in the casual way he had, straight ahead to the door. I was miffed at his crack about women and money, and I wondered what he had against Enzo. Maybe he was jealous – or just didn't like anybody. Looking back now, I see Charlie had a much clearer view than I did.

I sat there, hoping Enzo would show up and I could listen to his pathetic excuse and give him hell, then fuck him till he went weak. I didn't last long waiting. I wasn't going to sit around for whenever he got to me. Gary would be happy. He'd know I was home too early to have been laid. He'd think it meant something – I was back for him. I couldn't tell him I'd been stood up.

4

◆◆◆◆◆◆◆◆◆◆◆◆◆◆◆◆◆◆

It was only midnight, but the house was dark when I pulled into the drive. Gary's snoring came through the open bedroom window. No doubt he drank until he was knocked out. It was a relief. I got the door open without making any noise and stepped quietly across the terrazzo to the bathroom. My bladder was over-extended.

I shut the door before I turned on the light to be sure I wouldn't wake Gary. I sat down on the toilet and relaxed, let that beer flow. I smelled the smoke in my shorts and top. I pulled my clothes off while I sat there and flung them into the hamper.

As I stood up I saw dark drops on the tile leading to the tub – dried blood. I felt a shock run through me. I'd seen enough blood at the hospital to know it. The shower curtain was pulled across and I reached up and yanked it back. On the bottom of the blue tub was a bloody circle, draining into the pipe – a huge coiled snake – the head, smashed and severed, set in a position to bite its own tail.

"Jesus Christ!" I yelled. I stood there with my hand across my mouth. I recognized the pearl white, yellow-patterned albino python. It was Claire's, a neighbor I talked to at the pool. She'd allowed me to stroke its warm firm skin, and it rolled its hard smoothness against my fingers for a massage. I'd teased Gary about it, said I would like to feel it sliding between my legs. Now he'd killed it with his angry love, to let off steam. I knew that by instinct and I felt responsible.

I ran through the hall into the bedroom. I could see Gary from the bathroom light. He was still snoring, spread out naked on his back in the middle of the waterbed. I could smell his alcoholic sweat. I knew this was some macho gesture, like in the movies, to get my attention.

It made me want to sink a punch into his abdomen, sock out all his air. Instead, I pounded the mattress. I smashed down hard by his side, making violent swells to knock him out of whatever drunken peace he had the fucking nerve to be resting in.

It was too dark to see his eyes but the snoring stopped. "Hey, what the fuck!" he yelled. "What the fuck are you doing, Ramona?"

I kept on. I let the bed have it over and over, without the guts or the strength to touch him. I kept picturing that beautiful, helpless snake.

I couldn't look at him. I screamed in anger. He grabbed my wrists and mashed my face into the mattress with all his upper body weight on my shoulders. I was pinned. I couldn't get a breath. I tried to twist to my side using all my strength. I couldn't turn an inch.

I stopped moving and I thought he'd let me up, but he kept me there. I screamed harder and kicked my legs out behind me. My sound was a muffled squeak into the waterbed. I was trapped under his body. My lungs ached and my trachea burned.

Finally he moved off me. I gasped for breath. I coughed and lifted my head. He moved me around. He still had my wrists and he stretched them above me and I felt his penis dig in. It took the air I had back out. He seemed bigger and harder than I'd ever felt him, unbelievably hard and hot. I shoved myself against him and took it all and sobbed as my chest tightened in the most intense passion I'd ever felt, a passion like hate and need at the same time.

He came and pulled out and I rolled over and stood up, shaking and leaning against the bed.

"Are you fucking insane?" I whispered. I was panting. "Why'd you kill that snake? What the hell were you doing? That was Claire's pet."

He sat straight and rubbed up and down his scratchy beard, like he was trying to clear the fog out of his brain. He let out a groan and put his hand to his forehead. "I killed it?"

"Fuck. You coiled it in the tub, like some kind of sculpture." I couldn't go on. I didn't know what to say to him. It was too crazy, even for his being drunk.

"Shit." He was rubbing his forehead. "I forgot. I was sitting out back by the tree and it dropped down next to me. I didn't know it was a pet. I just stomped it on the head. I don't know these tropical snakes."

"Jesus. Why'd you cut the head off?" I asked. He wasn't making any sense to me. He wasn't that stupid.

"It kept wiggling, like it was in pain. I got the shovel and put it out of its misery."

"And then you coiled it in the tub? . . ." I stood there with my mouth hanging open.

"No. Did I? I guess I was waiting for you – to show you."

I took him by the hand into the bathroom. I pointed, then stared at Gary. "Spike," I said. I'd remembered its name.

He shook his head, looked down.

He still didn't remember or didn't admit it. I knew he'd done it against me, to show me how desperate he was, how much he needed me. I couldn't care anymore. The responsibility for his happiness suffocated me. "It's over for us," I said. "It's over."

"I'll buy her another one, next check I get," he said. His voice cracked. "It was a mistake. That's all." He looked at my face. "I'm sorry." He slumped down onto the toilet.

He was sorry, I believed him, so was I. "You can't buy another Spike," I said. My voice broke off in a sob, but I felt freedom within reach. "It's over," I said. Some tears started to slither down my cheeks. "If you want I'll stay here and pay the bills and you can find something cheaper."

Gary didn't move, didn't take his eyes off mine.

"We'll figure it all out tomorrow," I said. I walked out. My tears were streaming, but it was pain I had to get through to the relief on the other side.

I went to the kitchen for a plastic bag. I heard Gary go back to the bedroom. I took the bag into the bathroom and scooped the snake into it and carried it outside to the bank of the canal. I got a shovel from Gary's trailer. It had blood on it – the shovel he used to decapitate the snake. I saw blood every day, but this made me flinch.

I dug and sweated. I would wait to tell Claire in the morning. Maybe I could make the story sound less cruel. I wondered where I was going to get the money to keep up the rent and bills. I'd never lived alone, going straight from home to Gary, never had sole responsibility. But it was done, final in my mind, and I felt the freedom. I was ready for it.

I finished digging and put the plastic bag into the hole, covered it with dirt, tamped it down. It was a windy night and I started to cool off. I leaned on the shovel, looked into the sky, wondered what next. A perfect round moon slid out of the clouds. It figured. I was glad I wasn't working the emergency room.

I started to breathe the fresh air and notice the wind whipping my ponytail. Enzo slipped into my mind – dark, powerful, deep and simmering. I could blame him for all this if I wanted to. I inhaled deeply, let the shovel drop, and stretched my arms over my head into the ficus leaves.

5

◆◆◆◆◆◆◆◆◆◆◆◆◆◆◆◆◆◆

The next day was hell. Gary begged me to forgive him. He said our problems were all his fault. He was willing to do anything to make me happy, but I knew it wouldn't work. "I'm the problem," I told him. "It's all inside of me." His pleading made me want to tear out of there.

We spent the morning packing and crying. I was miserable for him and scared for me. When he left I'd be there alone, poor, stranded, without a car. It was still my choice.

I showered and got ready early for my three o'clock shift. I told Gary I'd talk to Claire before I caught the bus to work. He was finishing up to move in with a friend. Said he'd be gone when I got home.

I kept an eye out for Claire and saw her getting into her car in the early afternoon. I ran to stop her. She had on a black leotard and tights. She rolled down the window.

"Running late," she said. "Dance rehearsal."

"Your snake," I said. I crouched down and panted through the window. "It got out. I'm so sorry."

"Are you sure? I think he's in the laundry basket."

I put my hand on her forearm. I felt like I was stopping family on the way to an empty hospital bed. My eyes filled up.

"He's dead. It was late last night. Gary killed him – accidentally."

"Spike? White with yellow?"

"I'm so sorry. I was out. He didn't know it was a pet. It happened fast. Spike didn't suffer."

"I can't believe it." She wiped tears from her eyes. Glared at me. "Gotta go," she said. "Put him behind my place."

"He's buried," I told her, "in a nice spot by the water. Gary and I split up."

She swallowed and nodded and rolled up the window. "Gotta go." She looked at me hurt and cold. I wondered if she could figure that Spike was the victim of our problems. I watched her drive down the street. I should have invited her for coffee or something the next day, to talk.

I called a taxi for work and kissed Gary without a word on my way out. He grabbed me and held me and it made me cry, but I never considered changing my mind.

That night I got home to darkness and a hollow feeling. Gary's side of the dresser and his shelves were empty. Snickers came walking out from under the bed looking at me, knowing something was wrong.

I went into the bathroom and took my clothes off and crouched in the corner between the toilet and tub. I curled over with my arms clasped around my knees, my face against my thighs, the toilet bowl wedged into my side, trying to chill myself, to change into a rational woman. Gary would come back with a word. If only I could accept normal married life, make it my goal to have a good marriage, help each other. I stayed there a long time, willing my muscles to atrophy. I tried to give up all my wild notions, but it didn't work. I had seawater on the brain. Divers to explore. Enzo. Flowing freedom. Without a lobotomy, I couldn't change.

I woke up freezing on the tile floor and dragged my stiff body into the bedroom. I stretched into the comfort of clean sheets. I drifted back to imagining Enzo, picturing his dark furred chest, compact muscular shape, the indentation of his waist below the rib cage. Okay, he was a crutch to take my mind off Gary – Gary, I owed him a call. I fell asleep and dreamed of Enzo floating naked in an ocean of yellow damsel fish. His stiff cock flew a tiny flag, a black and white pirate flag, but I couldn't take the hint.

6

When I woke up in the morning, the sun was out. I felt rested and everything was shining. It was impossible to suffer in such a fucking beautiful climate.

I stared out the window, my eyes unfocused, taking in the glitter on the leaves. A huge monster of a lizard scuttled up the trunk of the ficus. The animal was only ten feet or so from my window, basking in the streaks of sun through branches. It was chartreuse green, about five feet from nose to tail, plump in the middle. Spines trailed from the head along the back and a dinosaur frill ran down the throat. I'd heard of iguanas living in trees locally, but I'd never seen one loose before. It stared at me past the coarse hairs that were ficus roots hanging from the branches between us. Its bright gold eyes glinted in a cartoon-character face.

I lay still and wondered if it – he, must be a he – was there somehow for me. A pet to take Gary's place? Weird karma. His eyes shifted. He seemed to be watching my face and trying to figure me out. The lizard didn't move and I lay there and stared back.

I knew how to care for an iguana. My friend Magda, up North, had one. Now the critter was dead – Saint Ignace. He used to climb to the top of bookshelves and then drop down on a coffee table in front of us, scaring me to death, sending cups and ashtrays into our shins. He enjoyed it. When Magda went out, he'd ride on her shoulder wearing his rhinestone collar, and she'd hold the end of his chain with two fingers, her pinkie sticking out like she was drinking tea. Saintly would cock his head dog-like, listening to the conversation. Sometimes he caught her with a whip of his tail across her face, but never caused any real damage. He could have hurt her if he tried. I wondered if I could tame this prehistoric creature to take a ride on me.

I remembered Magda putting Saintly into a pillow case to take him to the vet's, so I took one off the pillow I'd been clutching under my chin and slid off the bed backwards away from the window. I didn't want to make a move forward and scare him. I crouched down on the floor to pull on my shorts and T-shirt and tried to stay below his vision, moving slowly out the door.

As I passed the spare room I saw the shrimp net leaning against the wall – never been used. Gary and I were going to try it together, scoop shrimp by lantern light at the inlet, fill coolers with a slippery feast. Ha. A romantic idea.

The net had about an eight-foot handle. I wouldn't have to get too close to drop it over Ignats – I'd already named him. I grabbed the net and headed out the front door and around the side of the building.

The ficus leaves were damp and limp against the sand, so I was able to creep quietly as I came up behind the lizard. I dropped the pillow case to use later. He was still staring into the window, but I noticed he couldn't have been watching me. If anything, he was staring at his reflection.

I took a breath and planned my aim. His head was about chest high and his tail almost touched the ground. I figured I'd only get one lunge and if I missed him he'd run like hell up the tree, swift as the little anoles that scattered everywhere. I knew his tail wouldn't fit inside the rim of the net, but I hoped he would get his feet tangled and then I could push him in the rest of the way.

I raised the net, took one more step and jerked it down over his head. I wasn't ready for the fight he had in him. He twisted and clawed and wrenched, so I had to use all my strength to hold the net against the trunk and ease him down. I was afraid I was hurting him and I started to feel bad, to wonder if capturing him was a stupid idea. But he'd squirmed himself inside the net, and his toenails were caught, and I knew I had to deal with him one way or another.

He stopped moving and he was staring at me hatefully through the thin nylon of the net, building up energy for another spasm. I put the handle on the ground and stepped back to grab the pillow case. I stooped and dropped it over the net and slid it underneath so he was completely enclosed and then held the end tight as I lifted him and let gravity pull him into the sack. He knew the hopelessness of trying any more tricks and held still as I carried him around the building and inside. His body was strong and firm.

I figured I'd give him the run of the apartment. It would be his territory and maybe it wasn't a whole lot smaller than what he had staked out in the back. He must have been an escapee from a former owner, or the progeny of an escapee. Iguanas weren't native to Florida. I could rationalize taking him.

I remembered that Saintly had been killed by the cops. They drowned him in some macho display, as if he was trained to attack. It was all against Magda and her cocaine. Saintly was the victim of her addiction.

I thought if I saved Ignats I could keep him from harm. His climate would be controlled, and that alone might save his life in the winter.

I set the net in the middle of the living room floor and crouched beside it to untangle him. Snickers awakened from a nap and stretched her back in front of us, getting ready to see what was up. I pulled off the pillowcase, leaving him under the net. He was staring at me again, his left eye aligned with a round hole in the nylon. It looked like a gold bead in one of those plastic toys where you had to roll the balls into holes to add up points. When I was a kid I'd had one that I managed to break open so I could place the little balls with my fingers. It wasn't any fun after that. My mother complained there wasn't anything I couldn't ruin. I guess she was right.

I lifted the rim of the net and peeled back the nylon from the iguana's tail. Suddenly he began to lash it and caught me on the wrist, causing me to drop the net. My wrist stung. I knew I'd get a bruise. He was powerful.

I massaged my wrist and then started on Ignats from the other end. I lifted the metal rim and pulled the nylon off his head, grasping him around the shoulders with one hand and pulling the net down to his legs. I stroked his fine beaded skin, massaged the base of his neck. He stretched a little, a human response. I bent forward and kissed him on the neck, rubbed my cheek along his spines.

His toenails were sharp little needles and I had to lift toe by toe to peel them free. My hand on his shoulders must have convinced him there was no use in struggling, but I knew if he tried he could do some damage with those claws.

I'd barely untangled the last nail when he leapt across the room. Snickers sat up instantly where she lay, a few feet from him, and I was afraid she'd pounce. I lunged to get her and missed, and she chased him under the couch and let out a godawful cat scream. I dropped to my hands and knees but couldn't see under there to the corner. I listened to the hissing and thrashing and thought I might have dragged a beautiful creature in to die.

I started to scoot on my stomach to put my head under the couch when Snickers popped out and sprinted for the bedroom. I followed her and found her sitting on the window sill, looking outside. There was no blood on her mouth and she seemed to be unhurt, so I closed her in the room and went to check Ignats. I wished he'd never waited for me on the tree that morning, but I didn't want to let him go.

I peered under the couch, and couldn't see any damage on him either. I got up and went into the kitchen to find something for him to eat. I wanted to show him I was on his side. I remembered that Saintly used to like yellow squash and romaine lettuce. There was no squash, but I ripped into a slimy head of iceberg and came up with two good leaves from the inside. I took them to the living room and got down on my hands and knees again and squirmed half under the couch. He was staring at me, alert and ready to run.

"Easy," I said. I wanted to cuddle him to my chest. "Easy, lover," I said.

I reached under slow and placed the lettuce a few inches in front of his nose. He was still, but I could see his side moving in and out with rapid breathing. He turned and walked to the other end of the couch. I watched for a few minutes and he didn't move.

I had nothing to do so I put on my bikini and went over to the apartment pool to cool off. The area was deserted. I felt alone. I spread my towel on a chaise lounge. I walked down the concrete steps into the water. It was a rush of cold heaven that brought me back to life. I was free and there was a whole ocean waiting for me. What took me so long to think of it?

I grabbed my towel and ran into the apartment to call the dive shop and make my reservation for mini-season, the coming weekend. I didn't recognize the voice that answered. It wasn't Enzo. My blood pumped while I waited.

"No problem," the guy said. "You're on."

I wandered into the bathroom and took a shower. I felt better. I realized I didn't have to tell Gary. He wasn't sitting there on the toilet lid with squirrel-fish eyes, staring at me when I combed my hair, trying to drain me of the part he didn't understand. I was lonely, but I was free.

7

That week I spent all my extra time getting a car. I found an old Datsun and took out an emergency loan at the credit union. I was proud of myself, despite the difficulty of covering another monthly bill.

I woke up early Saturday with a tingle. It was excitement for the dive. The leaves on the ficus barely fluttered with a light breeze from the west, so I knew the water would be flat and clear. I knew I'd see Enzo.

I waved romaine in front of Ig's face to stimulate his appetite. He didn't respond, but I knew he wasn't starving. He'd eaten squash and monkey biscuit mixture twice during the week, but I wanted him to eat from my hand and cock his brilliant green head in attention to my words, obey me.

I took in his muscular shape and thought of Enzo again, the tapered waist, calves equal in muscularity to his thighs. Now that I was separated, the situation was different. If Enzo was interested in playing games, my availability might turn him off. If so, fine. I needed to taste life on my own for awhile, take control.

I had a spot on the afternoon boat. Charlie and Enzo were both likely to be working. They'd have gone out at midnight to get the first shot at lobsters for the season, and by afternoon with twelve hours of lay-up they could go back down.

I laid out my fins, mask and snorkel, de-fog, weight belt,

gloves, towel, log book, dive tables. I dug into the closet and found a hand net I'd bought in the grocery store, along with my lobster probe and gauge, and mesh bag for the catch. I'd gotten four bugs on a trip the last season and Gary had been proud. He'd taken a picture of the mighty hunter and her catch, and we'd eaten the tails with champagne by candlelight. I remembered thinking how much better it could be with someone else.

I knew I wasn't being careful enough with money, but I had to take $60 to pay for the boat trip and rentals, and I threw in an extra ten for beer afterwards. A beer with the guys couldn't taste better than after pickling your lips in saltwater all day. I figured I could treat myself this once.

I put my stuff into my dark green, powdery-finished Datsun, and it started right up. When I got to the shop, Charlie was there filling tanks. I checked in at the counter and signed my release, then walked over and flipped through the T-shirts. I had a thing for fish – alive, dead, painted, carved – I could look at them all day.

I was trying to figure out if I could afford a shirt with a colorful coral reef when Charlie walked past with a customer. He didn't seem to notice me.

"Hi, Charles," I called. "Going after the big ones today?"

He looked up like I'd distracted him. "Yeah. Hi," he said. "Be with you in a minute."

"Oh, I'm just killing time until the boat."

I moved my eyes off his tight little ass and the lean golden legs he moved around so gracefully on. I looked around for Enzo. It was getting to be a habit.

The guy called to me from the counter. "Ramona, you can pick up your gear now at the shed." He winked. "You're on the *Sharkbiter*, the little boat, okay?"

"Sure. Who's the captain?"

"Enzo," he said. "And Charlie's the divemaster."

Charlie and Enzo, a nice team. Ummm, I could feel the thought riding between my legs. I wondered if Enzo would have an excuse for missing our date.

I was issued a BC – buoyancy compensator – regulator, and

two tanks. I started on the first trip to the boat with the regulator and one tank. I wondered if I'd be the only woman on the *Shark-biter* that day. I hadn't seen any other women so far. It would be nice if I could get Charlie for my dive buddy – rather than some jerk who'd swim behind me and hyperventilate watching my bikini bottoms, his spear gun pointing in my direction. Those guys slurped air fast, cutting the dive short.

I walked over to where a few men were standing on the dock hooking up their regulators. Enzo probably wasn't ready for us to load so I set my stuff down and went back for the other gear.

He walked out as I lugged my second tank and BC past the door of the shop.

"Beautiful day today," he said.

"It's always beautiful to me."

He walked with me to the boat and I waited to hear something about the other night, but he didn't say anything. I didn't ask. I concentrated on lugging my heavy gear and left off the conversation.

The trip out through the inlet was a little choppy from traffic, but when we hit the open water I thought I'd die from so much beauty. I could feel my lungs expanding and my body trying to take in the space as much as my eyes. It was freedom, with nobody waiting to drag me back from it.

A song came on the stereo, and the rhythm of steel drums rolled across that flat glassy water and filled the universe with the beat of paradise. I knew Enzo had turned up the volume to create that moment. He was a man with the instinct for making memories.

Nobody talked. We all held the rail and stared out into the blue, letting our souls fly across the flat open space. I pushed off guilt and worry and felt all my concerns hit that clear glaze and spread out away from me like electricity from a lightning bolt. For a minute the delight could never end.

There were about twenty people on the boat, plus Charlie and another divemaster. Doug, the other captain, was there too. Everybody went out for mini-season. I told Charlie I didn't have

a buddy and wondered if he would be going down for the first
dive. He said he'd fix me up, but he had to work.

For the deep dive he paired me with Dennis, an enormous,
dark, bodybuilder. I tried not to stare. He was a hunk, and no
doubt too egotistical to be a conscientious diver. I thought he was
likely to dart away to get his bugs alone. I wondered if Charlie
was putting me to a test. I wasn't about to complain.

I sat down on the bench, hitched on my weight belt, slipped
my arms into my vest, and hunched the tank onto my shoulders.
I glanced up to see what Enzo was doing. He had a guy in
cut-offs with him on the flybridge, a scraggly blonde with a
permanent sneer who was talking. I felt an instant dislike. He
didn't belong in the pure daylight, more like in a dingy cell.
Enzo didn't seem to be listening to him. The engine drowned all
the words.

I felt my eyes slide down Enzo's hips, sweep the curly black
hair on his legs right above me. His gaze drifted down. His
black eyes connected with mine. I felt a twitch in my shoulders.

"Let's go, Ramona." It was Charlie. "Time to go diving."

Enzo cut the engine and I stepped up to the transom, sat on
the gunnel to put on my fins and mask, and stepped onto the
platform. Dennis was right behind me. I popped the regulator in
my mouth and took a giant step, into the rush of bubbles from my
legs. I looked to see Dennis whoosh down next to me. We hovered
beneath the surface and our eyes met as our hands went to our
BC hoses to lift them and press the buttons so any remaining air
would rip out of our vests. I stared at Dennis's arms, twenty per
cent bigger under water. He was something.

We drifted down in the clear gray. I hated to interrupt the
perfect silence with a loud slurp of breath and I held off for just
a few seconds – knowing it was forbidden – but I was safe on the
descent, unlike the ascent when you could burst a lung or push
an embolism to the brain. It was a thrill – having the power to
choose death. Every breath was a conscious decision when you
carried all your air on your back. Such an available way to die.
Everything was simple under water.

We dropped through a school of pompano, curtains of

flattened pearls gliding by on their invisible geometric planes. At once the school tacked and moved off together at a new angle, holding the exact relationship to each other and eluding our out-stretched arms.

I glanced at my depth gauge, saw fifty-five feet, and breathed as we touched bottom, having stopped breathing to pass silently through the fish. Dennis must have skip-breathed too because there weren't any bubbles. I neutralized my buoyancy by letting a little air into my vest.

Dennis pointed to a hole in the coral several feet to the right. I followed the tip of his finger and saw the thin pairs of antennae waving in the current. We'd nearly landed on a pod of four. Dennis had a good pair of eyes.

As the spotter he had first dibs on the pod. He knelt down to get a look inside and see if any other creatures had plans for this meal. Sometimes morays kept a lobster like a pet – till dinner time – so both of us knew better than to stick our hands where we couldn't see. We looked around the clumps of corals and I spotted an exit toward the left rear of the lobsters' little home. I positioned myself there to catch anybody who decided to head out the back. I squatted and waited for Dennis to work them.

I controlled my breathing, taking long deep breaths and letting them out slow to stay calm. His muscular left arm was pulling backwards inch by inch. I couldn't see the lobster, but I figured he was poking the biggest one on the tail, pushing it toward himself so he could drop the net in his right hand over it. His right shoulder dipped and he dropped the probe and I knew he'd made his move. He brought up the net and I saw a fine two-pounder tangled in the bottom. He unhooked the net bag from the side of his vest and I moved forward and helped hold it open while he twisted and pulled to remove the first catch from the netting. Dennis didn't pull off a single leg, unusual. I was surprised by his delicacy. Maybe he wasn't a muscle maniac after all.

He dropped the lobster in the bag and shook it down far enough so I could hook the clasp for him. It was a nice catch.

He pointed at the hole, allowing me to go for the second lobster. I lay down flat on the bottom to reach the next largest one. I put the prod behind it and began to tap the tail with the v-bent end. The bug came obediently like it was glad to leave the hole and I was suspicious, but dropped the net over it.

Dennis had come around from where he'd been guarding the exit and as I grasped the net and raised it he shook his head.

"Fuck," I said into my regulator. There were globs of crimson under her tail. It was an egg-bearing female who had so gleefully followed her mate into capture. It was illegal to keep her and I was sorry to have poked her, and now I had the difficult job of untangling her prickly legs.

I could hear my breathing using up time as I held her by the carapace and pulled the net away from her tail by spreading my fingers. She struggled as I picked each leg free, and I was thinking this was the second time lately I'd regretted capturing a creature in my net. This one's future was as prey, if I injured her. I had the sinking feeling of having over-estimated myself. The gloom lingered with me as I watched her dart backwards to the nearest cover.

Dennis tapped me on the shoulder. I turned and he looked at my eyes inside the mask. He gave the "okay" sign up close and I could feel a question mark behind it. I shot him a quick "okay" back.

He bagged the next catch and I made my second attempt. This time I moved my snorkel out of the way so I could squeeze my ear down into the sand and get a look under the tail before I tried to walk the bug out. No eggs. There were the little hooks the male uses to attach to the female. He was the smallest, but even so I could tell he would measure up legal. I tickled his behind and he began taking cautious steps toward me when suddenly he made a wild sprint forward. He aimed straight at my chest and I dropped the prod and net and grabbed with my elbows and then forearms as I felt him slipping through. Finally he was in my hands.

I laughed into my regulator. I could hear Dennis making the same kind of noise.

Even through gloves, the spines pricked my fingers but I got a good hold on the lobster's back. Dennis was ready with my bag open and I slipped my bug down inside. I had misjudged Dennis. He was the most conscientious and patient buddy I'd ever had.

We picked our way further along the ledge until he pointed to his gauge. He was down to seven hundred pounds so I gave a nod and we turned to go back. Enzo wanted three hundred pounds left in the tank when you got on the boat, or it meant a lecture at least.

We barely kicked our feet and let the current carry us back south toward the boat. I took in the wide view of the ledge and surrounding blue. Two black French angels with scales outlined as if in white paint moved in formation and picked at the coral. There was a constant scurry of fish nibbling and darting and flashes of light off their shiny sides. Such a peaceful and harmless-seeming world if you didn't stay too long or look too close.

When we got to the anchor line I checked my gauge. I still had nine hundred pounds. Dennis showed four hundred. He gave the signal and we started to kick upward, face to face. The current had strengthened so I grabbed the anchor line and went hand over hand. Dennis did the same. At the surface we put air in our vests and switched to snorkels. We drifted back to the stern fast.

I caught the buoy line and looked behind me just in time to see Dennis almost overshoot the ladder. I reached out and he grabbed my arm and pulled himself around so he could reach. "Thanks, bud," he said.

The others were on board and Charlie grabbed our bags, prods, nets, and fins as we handed them up one by one. Dennis waited for me to climb out first. He was a nice guy without trying.

I had just taken off my mask and sat down on the bench to slip out of my vest when Enzo came walking back along the starboard side from the bow. He stopped and called out.

"I need a volunteer – somebody who's still geared up and has air and bottom time left. The anchor's snagged."

I glanced up and saw Captain Doug at the helm. I figured he'd been at fault. Enzo was always flawless. Of course, his sleazy pal was leaning against the rail dangling a cigarette out the side of his mouth, and probably caused a distraction. I never saw anybody smoke on the boat before. I looked back at Enzo. "I've got nine hundred pounds of air," I said. "I'll go."

Enzo glanced around the boat, and I knew he was hoping for a guy, but nobody else said anything. Most of them were out of their gear and drying off. I knew Dennis had only a few hundred pounds of air left.

Enzo bit at his lip and looked at me. "It might be wedged pretty tight, Mona. I'll tell Charlie to gear up."

"C'mon, Captain. I'll give it a try. Charlie doesn't need to gear up. I can handle it."

He still looked at me. Charlie walked over.

I looked at his arms. They weren't much bigger than mine, just leaner. "The anchor was in the sand when Dennis and I came up," I said. "It can't be too bad. There were only a couple rocks around."

He agreed that was most likely the problem. It was a Danforth type anchor and the points could have gotten wedged. Charlie didn't have it off the bottom when Doug hit the throttle. I wondered why Enzo had let Doug pilot. Probably something to do with Enzo's sleazeball friend.

I put my mask back on, grabbed my fins and headed for the transom. Everybody was watching me.

I stepped in and dropped down fast, before the surface current could carry me too far. I hit bottom and headed into the current. The swim was hard, but I made it to the anchor without tiring. It was wedged into the rocks just like I thought. I gave it a yank outward, but it didn't budge. I tried hitting it sideways to jerk the prongs at an angle, but nothing happened. I tried pushing with my foot and I could feel how solid it was. Fucking shit.

I didn't want to go up and get Charlie and look like a wimp. I gave it a couple more pulls and I could tell I was using up air fast, with no results. I looked at the angle of the prongs and the rocks holding them. I took my knife out of the sheath and started digging in the sand around one of the smallest rocks. It seemed to be buried fairly shallow. I worked at it a few minutes and looked at my air. Shit. I was already down to three hundred.

I tried to settle my breathing and economize my movement. Finally I could feel some play in the rock I was digging at.

I pulled at the anchor. It moved a fraction. I looked at my gauge. It registered just over one hundred pounds. I didn't trust the accuracy. If I didn't start up, I might run dry on the way. I felt my breathing catch, my throat tighten. I wasn't going to panic. I calmed myself and gave one last long push.

I heard bubbles. It was Dennis. I'd been concentrating so hard I hadn't noticed him. He dropped down beside me and flipped a thumb toward the surface. I followed his suggestion, watching him on the bottom while I ascended, making sure not to rise faster than my bubbles, taking breaths and letting them out slowly.

Dennis put his shoulder against the shank of the anchor and gave one push. The fucking anchor broke free. He moved it to the side and finned up. I couldn't believe how easy it was. There was no way I could have freed that anchor.

I had my breath under control and I decided to make a decompression stop at fifteen feet, holding the anchor line, just to be on the safe side. I was right at my bottomtime limit. When Dennis got to me he motioned that he would continue on up. I knew he couldn't have much time left either. I figured he wanted to tell them everything was okay before somebody else put on a tank. I watched his sculptured legs above me.

At three minutes I headed up. The air gauge needle was on the line. I surfaced and pressed the button to put air in my vest. It did a short spurt and stopped. I'd used it all, gone way against the rules. Great. I couldn't wait to hear Enzo. I'd be lucky if he let me on the boat again.

I switched my regulator for my snorkel and let the current ride me back. Dennis was squatting on the transom and put his hand out for me to grab. He guided me around to the ladder.

I handed him my fins and stepped up.

"Good job, buddy," he said. As I whipped off my mask somebody started clapping. Dennis stuck out his hand and I put mine in it. "Thank you," I said. He squeezed my hand and for a second I thought he was going to take it to his mouth for a kiss.

"Teamwork," he said.

By then the whole boat was applauding and whistling. I felt my face go hot red. I tried to explain that Dennis had done the job I couldn't finish. Finally I just shook it off and went to my bench. I couldn't wait to get out of that cold heavy stuff. I looked up. Enzo was staring, his eyes piercing, lewd. I stared back. He smiled and turned to the wheel to start the engine.

8

◆◆◆◆◆◆◆◆◆◆◆◆◆◆◆◆◆

It was a ride through silk to the next site for the shallow dive. With teamwork we got three good-sized lobsters. On the way back in I sat on the bow by myself, letting my hair blow back and my legs shine in the sun and spray. The big day was almost over. I didn't know when I'd be able to do it again.

I saw Sperry boat shoes at my side and then Enzo lowered himself down next to me. "So wha'd you think of the dive?"

I looked up and saw Doug had taken over again. I wondered if that was why Enzo had brought him along, so he could goof off. "Loved it. I always love it."

"It's a shame you can't get out more often."

I wanted to say I'd gotten out the other night to see him and broken up my marriage along the way, but I didn't want to spoil the mood.

He smoothed his hair back and looked at me. He was less than a foot from my face. His teeth blazed white against his tan. "Did you ever think of taking a few more courses so you could work as a divemaster? Charlie and I have the Rescue Course coming up. It costs some bucks, but you could make it back once you get your certification."

"I can't. I'd have to take out a loan."

"Might be worth it. Dennis says you're a natural."

I took my sunglasses off and rubbed one lens with my towel.

He was watching and waiting. I took my time. "I'm separated from my husband," I said. It sounded loud. I wondered if the whole boat heard above the engine.

"Oh," he said. He frowned.

"You're the first person I told. It's only been a week."

"Didn't know you were married." He moved his eyes slowly from my chest down to my hips, as if something might have changed. "Good time to start some serious diving."

I wanted to ask where the hell he was the other night. I held back.

"Look," he said. I followed his finger across the expanse of glassy blue. There were two dolphins maybe a hundred yards away that had just broken the surface. They rolled in unison, silver curling through the blue.

"It's probably a pair," Enzo said. "They mate for life."

"Dolphins must be better than humans at relationships."

"Sorry. I didn't mean anything personal. It's just a fact. Staying together maybe isn't an issue – how much variety is there in dolphins?" He laughed.

I wondered why Enzo was paying me so much attention after blowing me off. Was it part of a game? Maybe he wanted me to dig for his excuse. I watched the dolphins as they turned and followed the wake of the boat. They seemed to be playing in the froth. One dolphin sprang up and skied the crest of the wake on its tail. The show lasted several seconds before it dropped down. "Unbelievable," I said. "I thought they had to be trained to do that."

"I've seen it before."

The pair turned out of the wake together, like they'd just taken a minute off from their busy schedule. They swam north.

I glanced up the coast. We were nearly to the inlet. Enzo said he'd better go back up with Blondie and Doug.

"Who's Blondie? A new captain?" I asked.

"No. Just a friend who's interested in boats."

"He doesn't look like the boating type."

He shrugged.

I pursed my lips and looked at him. "You know, you stood

me up the other night, but I'd still like to invite you for a beer when we get in."

"What?" he asked. "I stood you up?"

"You forgot?"

I felt my eyes seething. I couldn't believe he was trying that shit. "I was waiting for you at Seabirds. Remember? We talked on the phone."

He put his hands on his hips, smiled menacingly.

I blew out some air, deflated. "Never mind. I don't like your attitude," I told him.

"I need to help Doug." He turned and went back toward the ladder.

The boat docked and I got in line unloading gear. I couldn't settle down thinking of Enzo and his nerve. Dennis was on the dock moving tanks like they were styrofoam. He was a sweet guy. I should spend my time getting to know Dennis and forget Enzo. I watched the muscles move in Dennis's golden back. I looked up at Enzo's legs on the flybridge, the dark, hard shape of him.

I was rinsing my gear when Enzo stepped off the boat. He stood watching the scuzzy blonde drive off in a shining blue Camaro.

I took my time dipping my regulator and draining it, giving Enzo a chance to come over with an apology. Fat chance. He turned to me and frowned.

I dunked my regulator again and held it in front of my face to drain. His feet moved away. I almost called to him. He was just so fucking male.

I put my gear and lobsters in the car and decided to go have a beer by myself.

When I got to Seabirds some other divers were already there. I took a seat at the close end of the bar. When the beer came I took a long drink. Nothing could have tasted better, except maybe Enzo.

I wondered what he was doing. I imagined the feeling of his warm, wet mouth on mine. I looked up and he was standing there.

"I had urgent business the other night."

I felt my jaw drop. "Does that mean sorry?" I asked.

"I'm not sorry. I made a good deal. But I didn't mean for you to sit around and wait."

I looked at the trim pair of shorts and the nice legs coming out of them. "Okay. I didn't wait long. You can buy me a beer now."

I swallowed the rest of what I had – along with any idea of getting a real apology. Enzo sat down and ordered a pitcher.

I brought up the dolphins, how beautiful their skin shone in the sun, how I'd like to stroke one from nose to tail and wrap my arms around him and kiss his cheek – the spot where a cheek would be. "I've heard they enjoy swimming with people. Like at that place on Marathon." I winked. "Sometimes they get worked up sexually."

Enzo relaxed against the bar.

"Do you think they try to mount?"

"Probably."

"I wonder if a dolphin has ever penetrated a woman. I guess they could identify a female orifice by smell."

"Their senses are keen," Enzo said. "I guess everything's been done once." He laughed.

I wondered if I had a sexual glare in my eyes.

I put my hand on his forearm and rubbed my finger on a patch of dried salt. I wanted to lick it. I needed his frogman body to take me hard and fast. He didn't make a move.

"I need to get my bugs on ice," I said. It was my hope that he'd suggest his place or mine.

"Oh. You could've put them in the boat cooler. Sorry."

He paid the check and walked me to my car. I unlocked it feeling wetness and warmth and light-headedness, desperately wanting him to say "Follow me." He opened the door and I slid in.

"I have business this evening, but we'll have to get together some time." He shut the door.

I rolled down the window and tilted my head. I felt the steam rush out of me. I tried to look normal. I wondered what kind of business he was always doing so late. Probably getting down to business in bed with a different woman every night.

"Hey," I said. "You're sure a busy person."

"See you later."

I couldn't tell anything from his face – surely not a hint of regret. I thought what a jerk I was. "Okay. See ya." Fuck you then, I was thinking.

He watched me back out. It wasn't a perfect day anymore, but I let that part go. I had that beautiful dive locked away for keeps in my mind and the freedom for more.

I drove a ways and my hormones settled down and I started thinking about Ignats. He'd been home alone most of the day. Maybe he'd be glad to see me and trust me enough to eat something from my hand, or let me stroke his fine-boned rib cage. No chance. I knew I was trying for the impossible.

9

◆◆◆◆◆◆◆◆◆◆◆◆◆◆◆◆◆

I stopped at Publix and picked up some romaine, Ignats' favorite food. At least it was what disappeared the most. I also got a fried chicken dinner. I was too starved to fix those lobsters. I had to eat before I dealt with them.

I opened the door and took a look around. Ignats was out of sight as usual. I checked the answering machine, and there was a call from Gary. I decided to wait to return it.

I went to the kitchen and unwrapped the lobsters from my towel. They were still moving, so I put them in the freezer, to die in blissful hypothermia. I didn't like to stab them through their heads. I poured myself some wine.

I wondered if I would've had the same reservations if Enzo stood next to me at the sink ready to do the job. It was sad to admit, but I'd probably be sipping wine and hardly notice when he banged the knife through their skulls. Snowy white tails dripping butter and Enzo's tight Speedo would be my focus, not executions.

By the time I finished my chicken, the bugs were chilled into unconsciousness so there was no squirming or squealing. I put the knife tip between the horned eyes of the first one and gave the handle a thump with the heel of my palm to deaden his primitive brain. I chopped off a piece of antennae as I'd been taught, then twisted off the head and threw it into the trash. I did the same to the second and then ran the antennae up their anal openings to snag and remove the excretory tracts. They were equipped with the perfect tool for eviscerating themselves. That was something to think about. One of Mother Nature's little jokes. The process only required a little help from a human predator.

I rinsed the tails and wrapped them in plastic and foil to freeze. I was all prepared for a little celebration. I just had to find something to celebrate. Maybe the day Ignats would finally respond with affection. Maybe Enzo. Sure.

I took the romaine and crawled halfway under the couch to coax Ignats out. He sat there staring at the wall. I wondered what deep complexities his reptile brain was working on. I wondered what secrets Enzo had. Why was Charlie so negative about him? Whew. Enzo. I waved the leaves within inches of Ignats' nose. He didn't notice. Finally he turned his head and stared at the couch leg.

The phone rang and I scooted out fast in reverse. It crossed my mind that Enzo might have stood somebody else up for a change.

I was a little out of breath when I grabbed the receiver.

"Am I catching you at a bad time?" the voice asked. I didn't recognize it.

"Not really. I was just feeding my iguana. Who is this?"

"It's Dennis," he said. "I wondered if you needed any help with those lobsters. I meant to catch you when we got in, but you were busy talking."

"Appreciate it, but I already put them in the freezer."

"Maybe next time. You have an iguana?"

"Yeah. He's a picky eater. Hey, thanks again for saving my butt – and giving me all the credit."

"You did everything right," he said. "You just didn't have enough strength. You're a woman. I noticed that right up front."

"Cute," I said. "Really, I don't want any excuses. I need to be stronger, especially in the arms and shoulders. I don't like being the wimp of the boat."

"You're no wimp – believe me, but if you're interested, I could take you over to the gym. See if you like it. Weight-bearing exercise is important for women."

I told him I could make it early in the afternoon. I had my foolish mind on Enzo in some way. I didn't want an evening-type date with Dennis.

We set a time for Wednesday. At least I had a practical goal to put on my schedule. I'd barely been on my own a couple weeks, and sometimes I wondered why I was doing it. Sometimes I wanted to call Gary, just for comfort.

I went back to Ignats. I worked on him for twenty minutes, tickling his scaly nostrils with romaine and sweet-talking him, but he wouldn't take a single bite or even look at me. I wished he could be nicer – like Dennis.

I thought of something else to fit into my schedule – the Rescue class. I would have to charge it. I figured I could get some part-time private duty on the side for extra money. I just needed to call an agency.

On Wednesday I put on a blue sports bra and short tights to meet Dennis at the gym. I had the outfit from when Gary and I planned to start running together. That lasted three days until we had a fight.

I turned in the mirror to look at my gluteal muscles. They were firm and round, and my abdomen was tight and smooth. I had some decent biceps, but I needed to get stronger and more defined, build up my trapezoids and pectorals. I straightened my arms and tightened my triceps, squatted and checked my quadriceps. With my height I could be strong – with the right look on my face, menacing.

I opened the door into the gym slowly. A light odor of sweat hit me. It was the opposite of a hospital – a warm, dim germ-breeding atmosphere. It had a concrete floor and lots of mirrors, machines, and racks of weights lined up by size. About half a dozen men were working out on machines or lifting, no women; I liked it.

Short and tall, they were all built up. I caught their glances, either straight on or from the mirrors. I felt like an invasive item of curiosity.

Dennis wasn't there yet. I went to the desk, hoping I wouldn't have to pay. A huge blonde in a loose little pair of shorts and a skimpy, stretched muscle shirt came strolling over. He moved slowly so I had plenty of time to take him all in. Or maybe it was by necessity; the muscles on his legs looked too heavy to lift.

I told the guy I was there to meet Dennis. He said fine. He'd be happy to show me a few things while I was waiting. His name was Rory. I looked at his left nipple and side sticking out of the strip of shirt. His skin was tight and the muscles moved across his ribs underneath. He asked my name and said he could give me a good price on a membership.

I had no idea what was a good price, but I told him I wanted to build up my shoulders and back, especially my arms. He looked me over like a doctor, reached out and poked my right shoulder, squeezed my biceps.

"No problem," he said. "I bet you can start right on the bar. We'll see." He put his hand behind my back and walked me towards the row of benches. "You might have to build up to it. It's forty-five pounds without adding any weight."

He stood behind the bar and had me lie down on the bench and scoot up under it. I was looking straight up his shorts. He was wearing a jock strap. His skin was smooth and hairless all the way to the white pouch.

"I'm going to spot you. I'll hold on in case you're not strong enough," he said.

I felt him slowly letting go of the bar and I tensed and held it. "It's okay. I've got it."

He kept his fingers in place, but not touching. "Now let it down to your chest. Don't bend your wrists."

My arms were shaky and the pole dipped left and right, but I got it up and down a few times and set it back.

He straightened my wrists when I reached for it again. "Keep going to eight, if you can," he said. "That'll be one set."

It was harder with straight wrists, but I kept it moving in my lopsided way, and he helped me put it back on the posts.

Another pair of loose shorts appeared at his side, smooth legs, another jock strap. I looked up at the face. Dennis.

He winked. "I see you're not wasting any time."

"You bet," I said. "But I'm a wimp. I can't keep the thing from wobbling."

"That'll fix itself," Rory said. "Your body will get the rhythm and balance."

I lay there resting, fingering the cold metal bar. I could look up Dennis's left leg and Rory's right leg at the same time.

Rory looked down at me. "Dennis can take over. Let me know when you're ready to sign up, Ramona. Good deal on memberships right now."

I sat up and shook the hand that he stretched out. It was a soft grip, not at all what I expected.

Dennis showed me some pectoral exercises with the dumb bells, and then squats and dead lifts. He said I should alternate days working out upper and lower. He spent a lot of time on me. I liked the gentle way he guided my arms and straightened my shoulders. His fingers on my lower back sent chills up to my hairline. He was a hunk all right. Maybe I'd been wrong about who was my type.

He went off to do his workout and I tried a few sets on my own. I could feel the moisture covering me and pooling on my sternum. I hadn't expected to break a sweat working so slowly. Occasionally I caught Dennis's or Rory's eye from across the room. I wondered if I looked ridiculous.

I went back to the bench, trying to keep my arms straight and still when Dennis came over.

"That's enough for today," he said. "You'll get too sore and not want to come back."

"I plan on being sore," I said.

"Too bad they don't have a steam room here. That'd help keep you loose. I could give you a little shoulder rub."

I looked at his perfect, ripped body. "I don't have time today," I said. "I have some errands to run before work."

Dennis walked me out to the car. I told him I'd just gotten it.

"Nice wheels," he said. He seemed sincere.

I laughed.

He opened the door and then pushed the button down and stood there. "Will I be seeing you around here?"

"Probably," I said. I felt a twinge about the money. "If there's an easy payment plan."

10

◆◆◆◆◆◆◆◆◆◆◆◆◆◆◆◆◆◆◆◆

That night in the emergency room I forgot Dennis and started thinking about Enzo again. I was busy bandaging, hooking up monitors, handing out hospital gowns right and left, but I kept picturing Enzo and me under water.

I imagined us being a dive team like Valerie Taylor and her husband. I'd seen her documentaries where she wears the mesh suit and feeds the vicious beasts. Valerie never gives in to fear, even when the shark clamps down on her arm. She stays conscious against the bruising pain. I pictured myself waving a dead yellow-tail at jagged rows of gleaming teeth, tempting their power, making them take the fish gently from my hand. I pictured Enzo's gleaming teeth.

I pulled the curtain aside. A white-haired woman with skin like a crumpled brown bag opened her eyes.

"Doing okay?" I asked her.

She didn't say anything. It was better than a complaint.

She'd just been checked in and needed a bolus of fluids. I picked up her arm and felt the AC for the vein. The arm was almost weightless, skin loose and thin, vein fragile. "Let's find a good one," I said. I tried the other arm, went back to the first.

I thought of Cousteau, at the same age, the age he'd always looked – same skin, sinewy, but full of energy, at least on film. There was no reason I had to go the way of this woman.

I inserted the PRN adaptor, an eighteen gauge. She didn't flinch. She was used to being pricked and prodded. I set up the IV, adjusted the drip wide open, and looked at her face. Her eyes stared straight ahead.

I smiled. "Okay for now?"

She returned a grin, winked. She was strong, but bored to death.

I pictured Enzo and me in a shark cage together, dodging snouts and gnashing teeth between the bars. I would rather have teeth in my arm than an IV. Make life matter always. Bite back. I decided to visit the shop, sign up for the Rescue class. Wait and watch Enzo for a while.

The next day I put on some nice white shorts and a soft blue halter top held together by a knot in front. It was one of my sexiest outfits. I figured I'd run into Enzo at the shop. I was going to give him something to look at and act like I didn't notice.

When I walked in he was busy filling tanks with his back to me. I went straight to the rear where Charlie was putting wetsuits on hangers.

"Hi," I said. "Got any bargains today?"

He looked up and took in my outfit.

"No bargains, but everything's top quality," he said.

"I know. I don't have any money anyway. I just stopped by to sign up for your class."

"Great." He smiled and his eyes crinkled. The leathery skin in the corners made him look mischievous – like Ignats. He led me to the desk.

Enzo was glaring as we crossed in front of him. I smiled and said hi. He nodded, but instead of going back to work he followed me with his eyes. I ignored him.

Charlie filled out the paperwork and did the credit card check. For the combination rescue and divemaster class, including books, it was nearly a thousand dollars. Lucky for me, I had a fresh credit card.

He gave me my book and schedule for the course. I'd have to get Tuesday and Thursday evenings and Saturdays off work, but I could switch my shifts again.

"You have all your gear, don't you?"

That knocked me. "No. Isn't rental included in the fee?"

"Sorry. We figure by the time you get this far, you're serious enough to have your own stuff."

"Whew."

"You should consider it, Ramona. It's going to cost you a few hundred dollars to rent gear for all those dives. You could have your own BC for that."

I said I'd have to think about it. It was a lot of charging for one day. I knew it would be at least another thousand for everything.

The phone rang and Charlie picked it up. I was going to wait and say goodbye, but he was concentrating on somebody's long monologue. I saw Enzo look up from filling tanks, so I mouthed "See you later" to Charlie and waved to Enzo as I walked out the door.

I sat down in the hot car and realized how thirsty I was. There was a little bar on the corner. I thought I'd have a beer, then stop back and say goodbye or whatever to Charlie. See if Enzo was still hanging around.

It only took me two Coors drafts to make up my mind to get the gear. I went back to the shop and fished out another credit card. Gary had insisted we save credit for an emergency. This was one.

I waved the card at Charlie. "Show me your tanks," I said.

He smiled and winked.

He took me to the tanks and I pointed out a couple of aluminum 50's, the small size I wanted for easy carrying by myself. They were the deep pink of Ignats' tongue. "Wrap 'em up," I said.

He saw that I was there for the works and caught some of my energy. Enzo watched. Charlie took me through the regulators, gauges, and BC's, explaining the technical differences so I could make my choices.

I could feel Enzo's eyes following me around the shop. He was looking good in his tailored shorts and expensive Bahama print shirt. Even in my fever of buying I could feel some kind of energy off him. It was exactly what I wanted, but the power of his eyes made me tense.

I visited the compasses, watches, and gear bags and soon my selections took up the whole end of the counter. We passed Enzo on the way to the knives. I smiled and he nodded. I picked out an eight-inch stainless steel knife with a leg strap. It had a macho look to it. I laid it against my thigh. "Cool," I said. I winked up at Charlie and caught Enzo staring.

He walked over. "What about a wet suit? Twenty per cent off on a custom fit. You're going to need it."

"That's right," Charlie said. "The water will be pretty chilly in a few weeks."

I did need a wet suit. I was always cold by fifty feet anyway. I couldn't concentrate if I was freezing.

I motioned to the rack. "Go for it."

"We'll need to do a custom fit," Enzo said. "You're too tall for the standard."

"I always am," I said. "How much is that going to run?"

Enzo turned, like he'd already lost interest. "Only an extra hundred or so. Charlie'll fix you up." He walked off and Charlie went behind the counter and got a tape measure and told me to stand in the small mirrored alcove. "This gets a little personal." He laughed. "But somebody has to do it."

"Be gentle." I laughed and flipped my hair behind my ears and stood straight. I'd seen the procedure and personal was putting it mildly. I looked over at Enzo leaning on the counter. His mouth was slightly open. Nice lips. He was waiting. Charlie started with the arms, taking one arm measurement, then another, back measurements that tingled. As he went, he referred to a clip board and filled in the blank spaces on a diagram of a woman's body.

"Hold still," he said.

I giggled from a chill that made me twitch. I glanced over at Enzo. He hadn't moved.

Charlie measured waist, hips, armpit to waist, outer leg seam, more places than I could have imagined. I had to spread my legs wide for him to get the inseam. He pressed the tape with his thumb at the edge of my pubic bone. I wondered if he could feel the heat, but he was working fast. Finally he paused and stared at my breasts, tilting his head like Ignats. I was braless under my knit top and my nipples reacted.

He seemed to be deciding what angle to come in on. "I haven't done too many of these," he said.

"No?" I said. "You seem thorough." I looked at Enzo standing there with a hand on his hip. I felt giddy. I put my shoulders back a little more and tried to hold still.

Charlie took the bust measurement, sliding the tape over my breasts without touching, holding the tape together in back. He wrote on his chart. "Here goes," he said. He put the tape on my left nipple with his thumb and measured to the right. I was watching his face. He was squinting in deep concentration. It made me giggle again. Trying to hold it in made me shake. My tits bounced. Charlie took his fingers away. Sweat beaded his forehead like he'd been splashed. I couldn't stop laughing.

"I can help you with that, Charlie," Enzo said. His voice came from a few feet to my left.

Charlie didn't look up. He paused then put his fingers back lightly where they'd been on my right breast. I giggled.

"Give me that," Enzo said. He moved forward and grabbed the tape from Charlie's fingers. Charlie stepped aside and glared.

Enzo let out a snort like a horse and put his thick fingers firmly in place with the tape lying from nipple to my armpit. He tilted his head to read the vertical measurement like he was a pro. I couldn't keep from jiggling, holding a laugh inside, letting the air escape through my nose. His fingers were vibrating up and down with the tape. I was out of control and enjoying it.

"Time out," he said. He pushed the hair off his forehead and blew out a breath. He glared. I felt like a child being disciplined. I couldn't guess what he was thinking. Finally I settled down enough and he measured the other side.

"Charlie forgot to do your neck," he said.

My nipples were clearly erect under the shirt and the exposed skin on my chest was in full blush. I knew his light touch on my neck was not going to settle me down. I lifted the hair in a handful, held it against my head, laughed out loud.

He got the tape around and smoothed it with his fingers and the goosebumps rose from my back to arms and down the rest of my body. A sigh came out. I could have fallen right down in a heap with him.

Enzo's face was blank. He rocked a little on his heels as he finished making his notes on the chart. He turned and walked towards the cash register. Charlie followed.

I took a breath and followed Charlie.

Enzo handed Charlie the finished chart and stepped aside. He started straightening a display of sunglasses. Charlie tapped away at the cash register. The total came up $1,430.

I exhaled and handed him the card. "That does it for my spending for the year," I said. "I'll be eating a lot of pasta."

"Hey, why don't I take you to dinner?" Charlie said. "Hold off the pasta for a night."

It surprised the heck out of me. I glanced at Enzo. He was listening for my answer.

"Okay," I said. "I need to celebrate my new gear."

He picked up a tank in each hand and motioned toward the door. I grabbed my fins and mask, opened the door and followed him out toward the car.

"I don't get out of here until eight," he said. "You can meet me at my apartment – if you want. I know a great spot right there on the beach."

Charlie gave me directions to a small hotel that he was renting during the off-season.

We made another trip inside and back to the car. Enzo stayed inside.

Charlie whomped the trunk shut. "See you later," he said. He walked toward the building as I backed the car up to turn around. Just then Enzo opened the door and strolled out, holding something long, shining in the sun. I realized it was my knife. I'd left it on the counter. He had the sheath off and was feeling the edge of the blade with his thumb. He had daggers in his eyes to match. Charlie stopped a few feet in front of him watching.

"Hey, lady," Enzo yelled. "I know you're gonna need this." His voice was black with insinuation and I held my breath, waiting

for the rest, thinking he might be a psychotic killer. After all, I
didn't know him.

I rolled the window up. Charlie was between us and it crossed
my mind that Enzo might be going for Charlie. I'd seen what a
knife like that could do.

Enzo kept walking slowly. With Charlie partially blocking my
view, I lost sight of the knife. Charlie stepped backwards out of
Enzo's path and I put the car in first and looked up.

Enzo pushed the sheath onto the blade. He walked to the car
and stopped, then snapped the safety strap over the knife-handle.
Charlie stood watching.

"Forget something?" Enzo called through the car window. He
turned the knife, pointing it towards himself at waist level to hand
it over politely. I rolled down the window and put out my hand. He
passed me the knife.

He turned and walked back toward the shop without a word,
past Charlie. I was thinking what a fool I'd been to let him scare
me. Maybe it wasn't even on purpose. Sure, I knew I'd gotten his
attention.

When I got home I was starved so I sat on the floor and tried
to share vegetables and dip with Ignats, but he didn't eat any. I
poked a carrot toward his face and left it.

I took a minute to caress my smooth, pink enamel tanks. I
put everything together and partially inflated the BC. I cleaned
my mask-plate with toothpaste to remove the coating so it
wouldn't fog up. I put it on and looked in the mirror. Frogwoman.

I decided to start wearing my diver's watch. I could use it at
work since it had a second hand. I set the bezel on nine – Charlie
time.

11

◆◆◆◆◆◆◆◆◆◆◆◆◆◆◆◆◆

The phone was ringing as I stepped out of the shower. I ran dripping into the bedroom, hoping it wasn't Charlie with a cancellation.

"Why so out of breath already, sweetheart? Charlie just left here."

It was Enzo. "What?" I could barely control my anger.

"So you're going out with Charlie tonight."

I thought I heard a slurring in his voice. "What business is that of yours? You already stood me up once, remember?"

"Yeah. You come jiggling your tits around the store, I'm gonna be watching. Get it?"

"Get what?"

"The Great White . . . the Great White is waiting." He hung up.

My mouth dropped open. I laughed. The Great White. He had to be drunk. I shook my head. Despite the giggle in my chest, I got a tingle – a dangerous, excited feeling. I knew Enzo wasn't all bullshit.

It was exactly nine when I pulled into the parking lot of the aqua, two-level building where Charlie lived. It was a small, maybe forty-unit motel, in a less expensive area near Hallandale. I wondered if I could afford a place like it during the off season, live on the beach like I'd thought I would in Florida.

Charlie was freshly showered with his hair combed back. He was wearing shorts and a colorful T-shirt I recognized from the shop.

He greeted me with a kiss on the cheek and I walked past him into the small efficiency, thinking his voice sounded deeper, more sexual than I remembered. I took the beer he offered.

We sat at the small formica table with two plastic chairs. It was the only place to sit besides the bed. He had a nightstand, a dresser with a TV on it, and a concrete block and wood bookshelf he'd made for his dive manuals. I figured he must not have lived in Florida long enough to find out how roaches loved to lay their eggs in those blocks.

"I can't wait to use my new gear," I said, "and start your class."

"Yeah. It's a good class. Enzo and I make a good teaching team." He stroked his chin. "Part of why I asked you to have dinner was to talk to you about Enzo."

"Huh?" It was the most words I'd heard him put together and I felt a twinge.

"I mean I wanted to go out with you—don't take this wrong—"

"Okay. What about Enzo?"

"I just—I mean you'll probably think I'm saying this to keep you from going out with him—"

"No."

"He's not the most honest guy you could meet—he knows his stuff though—"

"Okay." I could feel myself blushing. My attraction to Enzo must have been obvious, and it seemed Charlie had only asked me out as charity work.

"I know you're taking this wrong, but I have to say it—it's downright dangerous to hang around with him. Don't get mixed up in it." He banged his beer down a little hard on the table. "Sorry. Let's have dinner and get to know each other. I don't want to talk about Enzo any more than I have to."

I considered going home right then. I didn't know how to take Charlie – whether to believe him or not. I didn't know either of them. I exhaled and brushed it all aside. "I can handle myself. I think Enzo's just a flirt."

We drove to a little restaurant on Dixie Highway for dinner. It was another woody, fishnet-draped place, similar to Seabirds, with red plastic crabs and fish lights hanging from the ceiling. Dusty driftwood was mounted here and there. I sat down in a dark booth and Charlie sat across from me. We got Buds.

He took a swig and pointed the longneck to a carved fish on a shelf. It was bright blue with a light pink beak and dorsal fins, and pastel yellow and pink brushstrokes across the body.

I looked, but all I could think about was Enzo. Obviously Charlie had implied a drug connection. It made sense.

"You know the parrot fish?" he asked.

"Sure," I said. "The ones that nibble on coral."

"They change sexes," he said. "Start out as females, change to males when they mature."

"Really?" I said. "Seems like it should be the other way around."

He laughed – as if I was joking.

I took a long drink. "Too bad humans can't try both—might help sexual equality."

"I'll pass."

"You could be somebody's wife."

"Like I said, I'll pass."

"Good answer."

Charlie laughed. He took a mouthful of beer.

I put my hand under my hair in back and stretched my shoulders. I thought I might as well try to loosen up – forget about the whole Enzo thing and concentrate on Charlie. I would probably be better off.

"There is an up-side to being a woman," I said.

"I'm sure."

"I was thinking of penetration," I said. "—being penetrated." I laughed at the look on his face.

Charlie glanced at the closest tables. "I wouldn't know." He took a drink and kept the bottle near his mouth. "Okay. What's it like?"

"Hmm," I said. I took a big slug of beer. "When it goes in the first time, it's a jolt. You can feel a tingling – stinging sometimes – and feel the skin slide as you grip."

Charlie's eyes roved again to see who was listening. I looked around in case of Enzo.

"Your hips want to rise, to slide closer, and pump harder, get filled up. You don't care what happens. You bear down and ride away, farther and farther, out of control, never stop—"

Charlie's eyebrows were up, crinkling his forehead.

I stopped to take a breath. "I wonder if it's something like giving birth. Except it's pleasure, not pain."

"No idea. You're way out of my realm." He finished off his beer in a gulp.

"Is it the same for men or—is it a feeling of power?"

"I never thought about it. No—not power, not to me."

"Well, tell me. What does it feel like—to be the penetrator?"

His face was pink. He picked at the label on his beer bottle. "It's warm—concentrated, I guess."

"Does it tingle?"

"I guess. Yeah." He was deep red. "But you have to have control. You can't just lose it or it's over. You watch the woman. It's like a flash of lightning when you let go—speaking for myself."

"I'd miss getting out of control. But that's good—the man can't for once." I laughed.

Charlie sipped. "You're a little out of control," he said. He was chuckling low.

"Ha! You've never seen me out of control."

"It's a scary thought."

I wondered if he was serious. He didn't have Enzo's nerve – but that was good. I was enjoying his shyness. "Sometimes I almost feel like I have a penis," I said. "Like I can feel an extension, you know?"

He was frowning. "Yeah?"

"I mean tingling and heat extending out. I figure it's like amputees who feel the missing limb – a phantom penis."

"Sounds like you've given this a lot of thought."

I laughed. I was ready to ask if he'd like to see me get out of control, but the waitress came with the food.

Charlie swallowed a big bite. "Did you know the male seahorse gives birth?"

"I've seen it on Cousteau," I said. "Looks painful." I held my beer up in a toast. "There's balance in the sea."

We shared a piece of key lime pie for dessert and Charlie paid. We were ready to go and I didn't know what he had in mind. I had plenty of ideas.

He parked in front of his room and I hopped out and beat him to the door. This time when he went to get us beers, I sat down on the bed and kicked off my sandals. The drinks I'd had were enough to make me take a risk.

He put some music on the radio, handed me a beer, and walked over to a little alcove where his answering machine was blinking.

He had the volume low. With the music I only heard voices. The first was a woman. Then Enzo maybe. For a second I thought he was checking up on me, but Charlie didn't say anything.

Charlie came back and sat down on the bed. I thought he looked pale. He leaned against the headboard and pulled his legs up to fit into the small space I'd left him. He started telling me what a good deal he got on the efficiency, how well the air worked. It was chilly all right.

I was in an awkward position like that, with him at my side and nothing to lean on, so I got on my knees and crawled up to the pillow beside him. I lay back flat with my hands behind my head. I wasn't sure if he wanted me there or not. I'd never lain in bed with a man who didn't start massaging some part of my body.

I reached across his chest and set my beer on the nightstand. I was tired of beer. I pulled my hand back and stroked the side of his face on down his chest to his neck. He was in the middle of a sentence, but I couldn't stand the suspense. "You wanna make love with me?" I asked.

He looked at me with a brow up. I didn't remember anybody having to consider before. I'd put him on the spot. Now I was afraid he'd say no.

He blushed. "I was waiting for you to ask," he said. He took
my face into his hands and kissed me. It was a light kiss, but he
moved around on my mouth nice.

I kissed back tugging on his bottom lip, feeling the heat come
up fast into my chest. I wondered if I was forcing him into something he didn't want. I put his hands under my shirt.

He started kissing my neck and I felt the sighs in my throat. He
began working downward with his mouth and upward with his
hands and I reached past his arms and fumbled with his belt until
he stopped to help me. I finished undoing the zipper and pulled
down the jeans. He wasn't wearing any undershorts. I was struck
by the marble white skin where the little nylon suit had been, the
small pink rosebud of his penis at the low point of the triangle.

I pushed him down on his back. He was nearly hairless with
only a dark blond fringe, and perfectly thin and compact with all
his tendons and muscles splayed out in front of me. The image of
raw frog legs went through my mind – with affection – and then
the clean underbelly of Ignats. Then Enzo, the great white. I
pushed him aside.

I lifted Charlie's testicles slightly in my hands and buried my
face in the softness of his organs, licking, rubbing with my nose
and cheeks. I put my hands on his waist and nuzzled and kissed
and stroked down his sides, cupping his pelvis. He still wasn't
hard and I wondered why he was slow to react, if he was purposely
holding back, or not interested.

I took his penis into my mouth and began drawing it out with
long solid sucking. His erection grew and hardened until I could
barely stretch my mouth around it. My jaws were tight, began to
ache. I was aching inside too, wanting him to penetrate. I was
ready to get on top when he lifted my face and turned me around
and put his mouth between my legs. I couldn't take it for long. I
wanted him, slick and hard inside me.

"Come on in," I said. I pulled lightly on his arms.

He wasn't paying attention. He kept up a perfectly timed
licking until I couldn't stand it any longer. My hollowness was
pounding on the inside. The mild tickling strokes of his tongue

were lost to the stronger need. I pulled at his shoulders to try to get him on top of me. He moved up and kissed my neck.

"Put it in, baby, please," I said. "Don't tease me."

"I'm not teasing," he said.

"C'mon."

"I'm not teasing you."

I didn't understand until I reached down and found that his erection was gone. It took the air out of me. I'd never run into that problem before.

He rolled onto his side and started to stroke down my breasts and abdomen.

"What's the matter?" I said. I was struggling with the empty ache between my legs. It made my words come out breathless, on the edge of hysteria.

"Nothing. I'm just not ready."

"Are you on medication?"

"No. I don't know what's wrong," he said.

"I have condoms in my purse," I said. "I forgot. Wanna try again."

"No, no, that's not it."

I tried to settle my breathing. "What do you want?" I whispered.

"Suck on me a little," he said.

I moved back down and took his soft penis again, pulling with my lips and stroking the base with my hand at the same time. It only took half a minute. He got hard as rock – blow job therapy fixed whatever was bothering him.

I tried to move up to squat down on him but he held me off and I gave in and went back to sucking. Part of his erection had drained, but it perked up fast when I put my mouth on him again and worked it. He pumped the bitter salty spurts into my mouth. I sucked off the tip and swallowed and cringed as I felt the burn in the back of my throat.

His eyes were closed, mouth in a Mona Lisa smile. At least it worked fast. I lay down flat next to him. It was a mystery to me, but I didn't want to think about it. He reached over, found my head and patted it. He made a low sigh. I expected him to ask me to hand over his cigarettes, but he started to snore. It was the most noise I'd heard out of him.

I lay there stiff, pissed off, waiting for my body to settle down. I started to think of Enzo, wonder why he called – the great white was waiting.

In a few minutes I was chilly and wanted out of there. I climbed off the bed and put my clothes on. I poked Charlie's shoulder and the snoring stopped. His eyes opened.

"I'm going to head on home," I whispered. "You don't need to walk me out. Just sleep."

"Thanks. Sorry. Rough day today.'

He puckered his lips and raised his chin and I bent to the side for his good-night kiss. He pecked, then looked at me. "I'm separated from my wife. Guess I wasn't ready for this," he said. "Sorry, Ramona." He smiled flat and put his head back down, closed his eyes.

"No problem."

"Goodnight," he whispered. He rolled onto his side away from me. He rolled back. "Remember what I told you about Enzo."

I shook my head. "Sure. Thanks." I left, closing the door silently, shaking my head again. So this was divorce – my wild new life. Gary never had that problem. It wasn't the best taste of freedom.

12

◆◆◆◆◆◆◆◆◆◆◆◆◆◆◆◆

I had my work schedule rearranged to fit in the dive class, but I hardly knew I was working. My mind would switch from the routine right into Charlie's apartment, replaying the weird night, or swoop into Enzo fantasyland – a place I figured was only safe to visit in imagination.

I pictured myself crouched above Enzo's muscled, amphibian shape. I had waves of sexual heat while I took temperatures and filled out forms. I hardly noticed bedpans and griping patients. My senses were occupied with more interesting ideas for the future.

On Thursday morning I jolted awake early with a feeling that I needed to get moving with my life. I had no more excuses of being held back by Gary, yet I was still in the same routine. I wanted to get full-time into the diving, and it seemed a long way off with the classes I needed and money to pay for them. But I was determined – if I could make diving my career, I wouldn't need much else.

I decided to put Ignats out for some sun. I'd rigged a bio-light in his favorite corner, but I was afraid he wasn't getting enough Vitamin D. Magda had always walked Saintly on a leash in warm weather or caged him in the sun for a couple of hours a day during winter.

I had a fifty-gallon aquarium tank I'd scavenged from the

dumpster and I figured I would put him in there with racks from the oven on top. His tail could curl to fit.

I knew he would claw me and I didn't have long gloves, so I got a pair of thick athletic socks Gary had left in the dirty clothes basket.

I closed Snicky in the bedroom, took the tank and racks outside, leaving the door open, and pulled the socks over my hands, up to my elbows. I crawled under the couch where Ig was sleeping as usual. I knew I would only have one grab, and if I missed he would be so wired I'd have to wait another day.

I put my hands above him, positioning so that I could drop one to his neck and one above his hind legs. I would hug him to my body, immobilize him, and press him into the tank outside.

I made my move and grabbed him in both places at the same time trying to slide him toward me on the carpet. He was caught off guard, but his right rear toes were spread and caught in the loops of the carpet. I couldn't move him without hurting him and I hooked my little finger under his thigh and tried to pry it up. I couldn't do it. The only choice was to pin him with my arm and use my fingers to pull up his toes one by one.

I worked four toes free and was pulling at the last one when he made his lunge. His tail whipped against my cheek and I was stunned by the pain. He tore from under the couch and clawed across my back and I could hear his nails hit the tile by the door as I scooted out backwards. On all fours, I turned in time to see him slip outside. Stupidly, I'd left the door open.

I heaved myself up and ran after him, throwing the door shut so Snickers wouldn't escape. He was racing across the parking lot where the closest cover was a Toyota. I sprinted barefoot across the grass to the asphalt just as he made it into the shade of the car. I got down and looked under. He was still, but poised and ready to run.

I thought about letting him go. It was probably the thing to do, but he seemed healthy and happy doing the same lizardly activities inside as he would out. Regardless, I couldn't let him loose in the parking lot.

I lay down next to the car in a thin strip of shade to wait. If I didn't watch him he might dash under another car and I'd have a heck of a time finding him. I didn't have a plan, but I was hoping somebody would come out and I could get help.

For twenty minutes I waited. Nobody even stepped out of the building. Yelling *help* didn't seem the thing to do – help, help, my lizard's under the car?

It must have been ten more minutes at least that I lay there watching Ignats, who didn't even blink. I heard a door open and saw a dark, medium-built guy come out of an apartment and look toward the car.

"My iguana's under there," I hollered. I pointed towards the right front tire.

He looked at me and started walking over. I wondered how much help he would be interested in giving a woman in distress if it meant crawling under a car in his perfectly pressed gray trousers and pale peach guayabera shirt.

"Is there a problem?" he asked, standing over me, his hands perched on his hips. He was a little older than I was, pale, with shining black hair parted in the middle and a finely trimmed moustache. His inflection and enunciation were precise.

"My iguana escaped and ran under this car," I said. "I can't take my eyes off him to get something to catch him."

"Oh dear," he said, "oh," and then he burst out in a loud hee-haw that didn't match the rest of him. I tried to keep my face normal.

"Wow," he said. "I had a dream last night about a big lizard. I thought it was symbolic." He hee-hawed again. "I see it was only a prediction."

Near my head, one soft, expensive shoe crossed in front of the other and his knees bent plié-style. Despite obvious insanity, he looked stylish and comfortable.

I looked up. "Could you watch him while I get a net from my apartment?"

"Hmm. Is it necessary to lie down on the blacktop? If so, I'd like to change my clothes. I was getting ready to go out."

"I'm sorry," I said. "I don't want to make you late. I can probably run him out."

"No, no, it's not important. Just tell me what I can do."

"Okay," I said. "He's under the front. Just stand back a little and watch. Follow him if he sprints." I pushed myself up, noticing the white socks still stretched to my elbows. "He's been catatonic for a half-hour."

The guy moved to the front of the car and stepped back. He squatted on his haunches. "I see him. He's beautiful." He looked over at me. "Cute Marilyn gloves, by the way."

I smiled with half of my mouth and then I took off sprinting to the apartment for the net.

When I got back outside the guy was nowhere. I moved away from the building scanning the parking lot, looking closely at the bushes to the left and right. Finally I spotted the black shiny hair to the far right behind a bush. He must have been bending down and stood up.

I thought, Jesus, after all that time Ignats bolts as soon as I'm out of sight.

I ran over. "Sorry," I said. "I never dreamed he would run like this."

"It's okay. I missed my jog on the beach this morning."

I looked into the bush but at first couldn't see Ignats.

"Right here."

I followed his finger and Ignats' beady gold eyes rolled up at me. He was perfectly blended into the chartreuse leaves and flickering shadows. "Okay, buddy, time to go home."

I reached in with my protective socks and put one hand on his shoulders pushing him down into a branch. I pressed my face into the leaves and twigs and wiggled my other hand up underneath his stomach to sandwich him between my palms and arms.

"Could you put your fingers over his eyes?" I asked the guy.

He put his hand and pale cotton sleeve into the bush and paused.

"Just cup his head while I pull him out, so he doesn't get scratched."

He put his fingers over Ignats' face without touching and tried to follow as I guided the lizard's body around the thicker branches.

It was slow going because he caught his nails on leaves, and his tail kept getting obstructed. It whipped as I pulled him free.

The guy jumped back. "He's an energetic rascal," he said.

I held Ignats close to my body and started to run toward the apartment door. I yelled thanks over my shoulder.

I managed to turn the knob and run inside and shut the door with my foot. Ignats was going to have to do without sunlight until I found another way. I put him on the floor and he charged under the couch. I wondered how far back this would set our relationship. I should have taken him to his tree and let him go, but I hadn't given it a thought in the heat of the capture. I pushed one sock down my arm and then the other and pulled them off.

I hadn't asked my neighbor's name. I stepped outside and looked toward the area he'd come from, but I didn't know which apartment.

I was sweaty already so I decided to head to the gym and sign up. It was a step toward my goal. I got another charge card from the dresser drawer and put it in my purse.

This time as I entered the gym I felt welcomed by the odor. I fit right in. I looked around at the sparkling machines and recognized the ones I needed to use. The feeling of being an invader in male territory had gone.

Rory was at the desk and two big guys were working together, down to business. I walked right up and charged the first three months and didn't even look at the total when I signed the slip. Whatever it cost, I needed it.

Rory handed me a card with the numbers of sets and reps and type of equipment and weights he'd set me up on the first time, and I took it and went to the first machine. I knew progress would be slow, so I worked hard. I wondered what Charlie would think of it. Probably not much. I bet Enzo would like the idea, but what did I care?

13

◆◆◆◆◆◆◆◆◆◆◆◆◆◆◆◆◆

I flew out of work the evening of my first dive class and picked up a tuna sub on my way home. I wanted to take a shower and get to the shop a little early. Traffic was heavy and I pulled into the lot at one minute till seven.

It was crowded with men. Charlie and Enzo were busy with gear, so I went back to the classroom and took a desk in the circle, where a few guys were already seated.

Everybody else began to drift in and I could see the faces register interest as they took in my legs crossed and stretched out in front of me. A couple of them let their eyes rove up to my face and back down, and I stayed perfectly still with my head propped on my arm, chin tilted up. I was self-conscious, but I could feel myself gathering sexual energy from the room. My breathing picked up until I noticed it and made myself settle down.

I hadn't figured on the concentration of male flesh and muscle that surrounded me. I sat there, feeling head-on and sidelong glances slide over me. I wasn't giving out any encouraging smiles, just taking it all in.

The men were dressed casual, most in boat shoes and tailored shorts with colorful T-shirts tucked in. They had expensive looking divers' watches, heavy on their wrists. Diving was a rich man's sport, but that didn't bother me.

I was just a lobster in a pot for the moment, but I could

handle it. I didn't make eye contact with any one of them. I basked in the heat. We were all going to play together, to enjoy excitement – even danger – for a legitimate goal.

Everybody was silent, waiting for Charlie and Enzo to come in. I could hear the low tones of their voices outside the door and wondered if they were discussing me. I pushed the egocentric notion out of my mind.

Finally they came walking in together, all business. Charlie introduced himself, outlined the course, and handed out the schedule of pool sessions and ocean dives. Enzo waited for his turn. He had the nerve to stare at my tits.

I passed copies of diagrams to my left. I enjoyed the casual sprawl of legs in my vision, the soft denim with the sex mounds so obvious.

Enzo stepped in front of me. I looked at his snug fitting jeans, the bulge level with my face. He squatted and his face was square to mine. He watched my eyes while his hand picked up a sheet of paper from the floor. It made me squirm, no matter how big an asshole he was, or maybe because of it.

He touched my desk for balance as he stood back up, and I could feel myself leaning closer. He stopped. Finally he straightened up and walked back to the front of the room.

Charlie finished detailing the steps to take in an accident scenario. He introduced Enzo to continue.

Enzo's voice came out deep. "I know some of you won't like this," Enzo said, "but there's no other choice."

I felt my heart pump.

"One of the most important lessons is the mouth-to-mouth. The only way to find out if you can do it while you're dragging the victim through the waves is to do it for real. What I mean is – you have to put your mouth over the other person's mouth and blow. You don't force air all the way into the lungs, but you have to keep the seal over the mouth while you're swimming."

There were low chuckles. Some of the men looked around.

"If you can't handle it, we can give you a refund now, but after we get started, you'll be out of luck. A complete rescue is required for certification."

I felt a goofy kind of power coming over me – my popularity was inevitable. Enzo was watching. I controlled a laugh. I visualized the coupling of moustaches and mouths. Likely none of them were gay.

In seconds all the eyes swept mine. I held a perfectly level gaze. Would I pick a lucky one or try them all? I was already high with the thought – warm sun, the gentle slosh of salt water, and my lips sealed over the mouth of a submissive classmate, keeping his head above water in the crook of my arm. So many options. There wasn't anybody in there I wouldn't enjoy putting a seal on. It was an erotic adventure laid out in front of me.

I looked around for Enzo. He was making an exit. I watched his slinky ass move in the casual way he had of walking that made me think there was a big cock leading the way.

14

◆◆◆◆◆◆◆◆◆◆◆◆◆◆◆◆◆

I walked into the classroom on Thursday night to see Resuscitator Annie laid out flat on the floor, no new Chris Clean male with replaceable jaws so each person could keep their own germs. I guess it didn't matter with mouth-to-mouth on the agenda.

The chairs were grouped in a double row. I sat down and flipped through my book. I could resuscitate Annie in my sleep. I was wound up.

I glanced at the door. Dennis had come in. He must have missed the first class. He smiled a big one at me and I grinned back and watched him fold his huge perfect body into the empty desk in front of me.

The seats filled up and Charlie came in. Obviously Enzo wasn't there yet.

The procedure was to read the section in the Red Cross manual and take turns in pairs practicing on Annie. Whoever finished the reading first would go to Annie and wait for a partner. I knew the techniques backwards, so I skimmed. I spent more time looking around the room wondering whom I'd be paired with.

I studied Dennis's curly dark hair, smooth neck and big shoulders and arms. He didn't look like he'd ever lifted a book, only barbells. He was flipping pages faster than anybody else, even the lawyer. I wondered if he'd read ahead or was faking it. Oh well, Annie had lives to spare.

I saw him reach the last page of the chapter and then flip back through. I closed my book and stood up, raising my eyebrows at him and motioning toward Annie. He nodded and got up, and we both turned and walked over.

I looked down at the poor unconscious girl with her closed eyes and wide-open mouth.

"You go ahead with the breathing," Dennis said. "She's not my type." He winked and we both laughed. Guys glanced up from their books. We sat down in position.

I bent to put my ear by Annie's mouth. "No respiration," I said. I pressed my fingers under her hard plastic jaw. "No pulse." I looked toward the ceiling as if somebody was standing above me. "Call 911."

I put one hand under her neck in the back, pinched her nose with the other, and bent down to give her four quick breaths. Dennis found her sternum with no trouble, spaced two fingers down, and placed one palm on top of the other.

"Now I recognize her," he said. He chuckled.

Charlie came walking over. "Start the count," he said.

We counted together while Dennis did the compressions, "One-thousand-one, one-thousand-two . . ." At five I bent and blew my deepest breath down Annie's throat. Her chest rose.

"Nice rhythm," Charlie said. "Now you can change positions."

"Good, I like being on top," Dennis whispered.

"This time only," I whispered back. I laughed.

He smiled and I saw his beautiful healthy teeth beneath the fringe of moustache.

I glanced up and saw Charlie looking stern. "This has to be done by the book," he said.

Enzo came up to stare. I hadn't seen him come in.

I moved down to Annie's torso without making a reply and Dennis moved up to her head and gave his four breaths.

"Nope." Charlie motioned him out of the way and sat down by the head. "You haven't checked respiration and pulse yet." He put his head by her face to listen.

"Sorry. I thought we were just continuing the process," Dennis said.

I wondered if Charlie was doing some male territory thing. I'd expect it from Enzo, but not him. I looked over to see what Enzo was up to. He'd moved off to the corner, talking to the lawyer.

Charlie moved out of the way and Dennis sat down and began the process over. I had no idea what Charlie wanted.

Dennis and I finished and walked toward our seats. "I saw you slip Annie the tongue," I whispered.

He chuckled in the low way he had. "I think I'm in love."

"Men always go for the dummies," I said.

I laughed and looked over right into Charlie's eyes, but I was having too much fun to care about his hard-ass routine. I motioned toward Annie who was being fondled as the next guy tried to locate her sternum. "She's already replaced you," I said to Dennis.

Charlie called out the next chapter we should begin reading. I glanced at the familiar diagrams of pressure points.

Dennis stood up and motioned for me to follow him out the side door to the parking lot.

He leaned back on the brick wall with his shoulders and the sole of one shoe and offered me a piece of gum.

I shook my head and stared at the muscles below the short sleeves of the T-shirt.

He unwrapped the gum and put it into his mouth. "I have something I have to do tonight, but maybe after next class we can go out for a beer. What do you think?"

"Sure. But what about Annie?" I was kidding around, stalling. I felt uncomfortable thinking of Charlie watching. I needed to untangle whatever I'd started up with him.

"Huh?"

I jerked a thumb toward the classroom and put on a serious tone. "I thought you and Annie really hit it off."

"Oh. We're through. She let every guy in the class paw all over her."

"Maybe she's not such a dummy," I said.

Dennis laughed and smoothed his moustache. "What about Charlie? He's keeping an eye on you."

"You think so?" I was surprised Dennis had noticed anything. "He's afraid we're having too much fun in his class."

He flashed his teeth in a grin. "We can try."

I told him I'd think about going for the beer next time, depending on my work schedule. We stepped back inside. Charlie looked up from Annie and frowned. I wasn't sure what it meant, but it was irritating.

Going through the procedures was like sleepwalking for me, but I enjoyed working on Dennis. I reached for Dennis's femoral artery, demonstrating the pressure point. My hand was on his cotton shorts side by side with his penis and scrotum, and I saw his eyelids flicker. He had those droopy bedroom lids with long dark lashes. He was so still I wondered if he was concentrating to keep from getting a hard on.

As I gathered up my books and purse at the end of class, Charlie walked over. Dennis was a few steps ahead of me outside the door, waiting to walk me to the car.

"Hang on a minute," Charlie said. "You feel like having a beer?"

I was shocked. "I can't." The words came out fast. I saw Charlie's eyes move toward the door, wondered if he just wanted to compete.

"Another time, okay?"

"Yeah," he said.

"See you next class," I said. I turned to walk out past Dennis.

"I'll call you," Charlie called, louder than necessary. He moved inside. Enzo was right there too, looking animal.

I turned back to Dennis. He'd heard Charlie. As we walked through the parking lot, I shook off the feeling that I should make explanations. Dennis had no reason to expect anything from me. Neither had Charlie – or Enzo. I had a feeling they all did though.

15

◆◆◆◆◆◆◆◆◆◆◆◆◆◆◆◆◆

The next evening when I got home from work there was a message from Dennis on my machine. Also one from Gary. Dennis said he was looking forward to Saturday's beach dive and hoped I would keep the afternoon open so we could have lunch. I didn't know whether I wanted to see him or not, but I saved the recording of his soft voice. I took a big breath and called Gary back. Luckily he wasn't home. I left a message saying I hoped he was doing well.

Saturday I woke up to beautiful sun streaming through the ficus branches. The leaves were still and I had hopes of another glassy summer ocean, gentle rescues sliding through the clear blue.

It was about 7:30 when I pulled into the parking lot at the beach. I was a half hour early so nobody else was around. I made two trips back to the car, carrying a tank in each hand on the second trip back. I was glad I'd bought little 50's. I wasn't even breathing hard.

"Early bird gets the worm."

I twitched and tried to cover it with my move to place the tanks upright next to my towel. I made sure they were sitting firmly, and turned. Charlie was standing behind me with a gear bag on each shoulder. I focused on the bulge in his white nylon swim trunks until I realized what I was doing.

I made a broad motion toward sky and water. "I just thought I'd enjoy the view before you put us to work," I said. "We couldn't ask for a better day."

"Yeah. You better put on a T-shirt or you'll get burned. We're going to be on the surface for two to three hours."

He was running his eyes over my bikini. Probably ready for another blow job.

I bent over to push the strap of my BC down on my tank and imagined the view from the rear. I felt the thin fabric pulled tight between my legs as I strapped the tank to the BC securely. Charlie was quiet behind me.

I picked up my regulator and attached it to my tank. I could still feel Charlie's eyes and I wondered if he was going to stand there all day. I opened the valve and watched the needle on the air gauge swing up to 3,000 p.s.i. I took a breath from the regulator and tasted sharp rubber.

I motioned to Charlie's gear and bent to set my mouthpiece on the towel. "Need some help?'

He stepped over my regulator and his face was nearly touching mine. I could smell his mouthwash. I took a step backward to breathe some fresh air. His hand came up under my hair and rested on my neck. He pushed his lips against mine and I felt the warmth and slippery softness. His left hand held my waist with the fingers inside my bikini bottoms. The thought came to move away but it never turned into action.

He stopped. He was facing the parking lot. "Here comes the crowd," he said.

I should have taken that moment to tell him I wasn't interested in getting together with him again, but I let it go by. It was going to be a tough day between Charlie, Dennis, and Enzo, at least in my own mind. I'd be lucky not to drown.

Dennis started onto the sand carrying his gear bag and I wondered if he guessed what we were doing from my blush.

"I'll call you," Charlie said. He took off toward the parking and passed Dennis with a nod.

I shrugged him off and took a breath. Dennis walked up. I could feel a twitch hanging between my shoulder blades.

"Great day, isn't it?" I said. I glanced at the sky to make sure no black clouds had sneaked up while I was occupied with Charlie.

Dennis dropped his bag near mine. "I'm already thinking of this evening," he said. He looked up at the sky and out to sea. "It'll do."

I managed to give a big grin. "Let's go diving!" I boomed. It was sort of an inside joke, mimicry of the new guys and their enthusiasm – but really the excitement never wore off any of us.

The first practice was taking turns dragging each other through the water, giving mouth to mouth. Charlie and Enzo hovered in the area while each of us practiced getting a hold on our partners and putting them in the do-si-do arm position to tow them through the water during respiration. Charlie moved up closer to observe us and sent Enzo to another group. Dennis told me to take my turn first and he lay still on his face using his regulator.

I approached and turned him over by the vest, then with his chin, leveled him on the water. He pulled out his regulator and let it bubble with free-flow to his side, where it stopped.

"Dropping the weight belt," I called out to nobody, as we'd been told to do, and pretended to undo the clip and let it go. I sputtered and treaded water hard trying to keep him flat as I pulled out his BC hose and blew in a few breaths to inflate the vest enough to get his face above the wavelets. I took off his mask and snorkel and handed it to him and pushed my own down around my neck.

"Checking respiration," I said and looked for a bluish skin tone and put my ear near his mouth, thinking I couldn't really tell if he was breathing or not with the slosh of the water. I grasped the shoulder section of his vest and pulled his face toward me. He stayed limp with his mouth slack and expressionless, and I thought how relaxed he was, trusting that I wouldn't let a ripple roll over his face. His wet-lashed eyes watched me.

Even the slight undulation of the water was a nuisance for trying to manipulate myself and him and not to break contact or look like I was having a problem.

I tried to keep my movements smooth as I put my face up to his. The water was just cool enough around us so I could feel the warmer air of his breath as I came close. I tasted salt and a sweetness as I held myself tight against his shoulder and engulfed his lips. Salty and sweet, warm and cool, hard and soft, I was wallowing in all the sensations of him and the ocean. Positioned as if for a kiss, I felt self-conscious of my mouth over his cool lips as I pushed a breath to fill up his cheeks.

Dennis's cheek touched mine and then I felt a swift current on my leg and realized Charlie was finning so close he must have almost kicked me. I started thinking maybe he wanted to do a threesome. Ha. I could handle the two of them, no problem.

"Tow him. Swim slow and keep the seal," Charlie said.

I kept the seal tight, and started the side-stroke kick pulling from behind instead of forward. My body was performing more actions at one time than I ever thought it could, with my mind floating away into the soft warmth of Dennis's lips above the cool water, and all the time aware of Charlie's eyes and his judgment. I figured I might have a seizure if my body was forced to endure so much stimulation and control much longer.

"That'll do. Switch," Charlie called.

It was my turn to be victim. I took my lips off Dennis with as much of a lingering look as I could dare and relaxed. He followed the steps and soon I felt his moustache brush my nose and his warm wet mouth cover mine.

He filled my cheeks with air so Charlie could get a good look. Enzo finned up and stared alongside him. All I wanted was more and more of that mouth. I was wishing Dennis would slip me the tongue in front of them both. Enzo would enjoy it, I'd bet. My mind was stuck right there.

Charlie and Enzo finally eased back to check on the other divers. Dennis and I kept practicing. I took another turn on top and this time I slipped him my tongue. It was like second nature at that point. His eyes opened up and he pushed my tongue out of the way and filled my mouth with his. I sucked on it hard. The water was like soup and I thought with my extra body heat it might start to simmer. It seemed the sexual heat increased because we weren't supposed to be thinking about it – like laughing in church. I knew he must have a hard-on somewhere down there, but I couldn't get in a position to feel it. There was too much gear between us.

It was after one when we finished the class. We were both starved. He drove and we grabbed a table at a Cuban cafe nearby.

"Nice place, huh?" Dennis said.

"Uh huh," I said. I had no idea whether he meant it or not.

"I don't know if I'm hungrier or hornier. What about you?"

"I'm already close to an emergency state for both," I said. "Being a nurse, I can tell."

When the food came we both went into a feeding frenzy. It was great stuff. I think. I swallowed my last bite and Dennis picked up his mug and took a big gulp. He looked at me and his smile made crinkles around his eyes.

On the way to his place Dennis warned me that he lived cheap. He was back in school working on a degree in Marine Biology. His roommate owned the house and used the bedroom, so Dennis slept in the living room. The roommate was out when we got there. Dennis put a seal on my mouth and we dropped down onto an open sofa bed surrounded by cats. My blood shot instantly to boiling after those hours of foreplay.

We unlocked for a few seconds to pull off our clothes. I glanced around. Big gold and green eyes looked me over like I was in their territory. A white ferret slipped out from under the couch and romped into the kitchen.

"Cute pets," I told Dennis. "Are they all yours?"

"They think they are." He sat down to put a hand behind my head and smoothed my hair. I tilted my head back and looked into his eyes. I didn't mind being petted for the moment.

Dennis stood and pulled the trunks off his firm upright cock. It was a beauty like the rest of his parts. He sat and I straddled him. I lowered myself onto the hard sting of a perfect fit, sending my mind into that place of no thought, no control, never needing to think again. I bounced back and forth from there to his eyes.

I came back to earth and realized we'd rolled over and I was on the bottom. I saw the cats had spaced themselves around us on the bed and were sleeping or licking. Dennis slid himself all over me, smearing every part of his body against mine. Hot waves radiated from his penis inside me. We were soaked with sweat, and salty as we'd been all afternoon, mixing our juices, diving into each other as deep as we could go, submerging. I was barely conscious of faraway moans coming from my lips. It went on and on.

I woke up still on top of him and rolled to his side under his arm and closed my eyes. I felt comfortable and cool in the evening air. I thought about the iguana and Snickers and knew they were waiting for me. I made a mental note to get myself up in a few minutes to go home. I thought of Charlie and Enzo and how much they didn't matter.

Dennis turned to me and I was on his mouth again. We started all over. I didn't wake up again until it was light. He was asleep naked on top of the sheet, his hair wild on the pillow. I reached behind my head and felt a mat of hair dried together from the squirming and sweating. I guessed the roommate hadn't come in. I stretched my arms straight up and watched my hands floating, feeling weightless. I felt cool in the breeze of the ceiling fan.

"Are you trying to levitate?" Dennis asked.

"You open your eyes and come up with a word like that?"

"I could levitate myself," he said. "That's how good I feel."

"We should be sore," I said. "Half dead." I put down my arms and raised both legs. They felt weightless too. "We really worked out yesterday – from dawn to dawn almost."

"So you think we have to pay a price?"

"No. I just mean we surpassed ordinary humans."

"You got that right." He put his fingers on my thigh, pushed that leg to the bed and then the other.

"I hope there's no price," I said. I felt my vagina stir.

"Maybe I should charge you." He put his leg over to straddle me and took my hands in his and held them above my head on the pillow.

"Uh huh. Maybe."

He put his head down to my neck and started to suck and nuzzle. "I think I'll make you pay right now."

"Mmm." His mouth was making me squirm. My hips were lifting.

"Yeah?" He slipped inside me. "Are you gonna pay up?" he said.

I could feel myself gushing, him sliding in and out all the way, hitting hard. "Yes," I said. "No, I mean."

He was pumping fast. "No?"

"Yes. No. I mean, it's good." I'd lost track of the questions. I couldn't be bothered.

"So," he said, breathing hard, "is it fair?"

"What?" I could feel little explosions all around my head, my vagina slick and tight on him. My arms tight, fingers clenched.

"Life."

"What?" I couldn't hear for all my breathing.

"Should you pay?"

"Mmm, yes. Oh, God . . . oh, yes." I came, again, again. I felt myself throbbing, bearing down against him as hard as I could. I grabbed at him, shuddered.

"Oh?" He held still, but didn't pull out.

I was panting. I got a breath, another. "What are you talking about?"

"I'm just dickin' with you."

"No, you're not."

"I'm not dickin' you?" He started to move again, push deep.

"Mmm. No, not just."

"I'm not just?"

"Not just dickin', I mean." I was feeling it again, the speed picking up and my hips following and spreading pulses of heat up to my head, little explosions. It was interesting trying to think and talk at the same time.

I watched him reading the pleasure in my eyes and I kept coming. I watched his face. His jaw slackened. He hardened even more and I knew he was coming and I came again all over him. We were smooth machines.

It was ten by the time we showered and went out to breakfast. I felt guilty going home so late to feed the animals. I knew they were feeling empty and wondering where I was. Dennis said we had a dive the next Saturday and could do it all again. It was wonderful, but I backed out of his drive hoping he didn't want to

get too serious. I'd barely started on my freedom. I thought of
Enzo and felt guilty. When I moved my eyes down from the
rearview mirror Dennis had gone inside.

I picked up some squash for Ignats on the way home. It was
noon as I walked in. I saw the blinking light on my answering
machine, but Snickers jumped up on the counter top to be fed so
I went to her first. Ignats was on the window sill across the living
room for a change, posed like a miniature dinosaur, lime green
and beautiful.

I mixed the food and put the dish in front of Ig's face. He
flicked his tongue and touched the yellow edge of one tiny piece
of squash. I waited. His eyes rolled around and I knew he was
studying me and I remembered the bead-in-the-hole game his eye
had first reminded me of. His eye rolled. He sneezed. A wet one.
I felt the spray of mucus on my forearm. He stared. I stood there
waiting, waiting for something. He didn't move.

I put the dish on the sill and went to check my messages.
There were three. Charlie's voice came in loud and jolly. He had
called in the evening. He wanted to get together.

The machine beeped for the second message and there was a
throat-clearing noise. "It's Enzo. Remember me. Good old Enzo.
The only diver you're not fucking."

He was still drunk or drunk again. "This is Enzo – the one
you don't talk to because you're too busy fuckin' all his friends?
Enzo. What? Can't talk? What're you doin'? You in the middle
of fucking one of my friends right now?" He was talking rapid-
fire. "Let me guess – Charlie? No? Dennis? Hey, Dennis, can you
hear me?"

I took the phone away from my ear and I could still hear him
yelling. "Denny, hey, Den? Do 'er one for me, buddy!"

I put the receiver down by my side until I heard the beep for
the next message.

The next voice was Dennis, slow, cool. "Hi, beautiful. Just
called to say I'm sore." He paused. The machine cut off. He must
have called already while I was on my way home. I wondered
what else he would have said if he'd had time to think about it.
He was sweet. It made me a little nervous.

I erased all the messages to get rid of Enzo's. I felt my stomach contracting. He had a point about my fucking, but I hadn't planned any of it. I told myself that I shouldn't care. Enzo was an asshole. I knew that. But there was something between us that I couldn't figure out enough to fight off.

16

◆◆◆◆◆◆◆◆◆◆◆◆◆◆◆◆◆

I didn't get around to calling Charlie back that week. I guess I was just hoping he'd let it go. It was easy to put him out of my mind – all my extra time was taken up in the gym. Rory had me on a heavy schedule and kept me pumping hard. He enjoyed torture. Dennis called on Wednesday and said to bring clothes after the class on Saturday – he'd like to take me to a nice restaurant. I knew we'd be finishing up in the afternoon, so there would be hours to fill before dinner. Sounded like a good plan to me.

Saturday was scheduled as a boat dive with the same rescues we had performed off the beach, except this time we'd be in about thirty feet of water and would go through the whole scenario, bringing the victim up from the bottom, dragging the body onto the boat and simulating CPR and emergency radio calls.

That morning I woke up to cloudy skies and mild anxiety. I figured it was about seeing Charlie. My second thought was Enzo, and I really started to sweat. I needed to tell him just what an asshole he was. Finally I set my mind on the dive and decided I wasn't going to worry about either of them. They were professionals and wouldn't let anything interfere with their teaching.

As I drove toward the water, the wind from the east picked up. It wasn't going to be the flat ocean we'd had on the previous dives.

Charlie was on the boat alone when I pulled up, so I walked over, glad to have something to ask that would delay talk about us. He was drawing a diagram on the blackboard, frowning.

I put my tanks on the ground and he heard the clunk and turned around.

"Ramona," he said. He was still frowning. "It's a little rough today for rescues. Seas up to four feet." He looked hard at my face. "Think you can handle it?"

"You tell me," I said. "I can if the others can."

"I thought I'd ask you first."

"Are you thinking of calling off the dive?" I asked. I wasn't about to be the one to blame.

He looked at me annoyed and I thought that was just what he wanted, me to blame.

"I'm up for it," I said, "if you're taking a vote." I turned and walked towards the shop. I decided to get some Triptone. I wasn't going to get seasick.

Dennis pulled up across the lot so I hurried to the shop. I didn't want to meet him in front of Charlie, in case he'd kiss me. Enzo was standing right there when I opened the door. He looked as surprised to see me as I felt, nearly walking into him. I'd forgotten how dark his eyes were.

"Enzo," I said. His name came out softer than I intended, lingering. I couldn't think what else to say.

"Ramona. I'm sorry – for the phone call. I didn't know I was gonna blow up like that. I just called to see what was going on – I had too much to drink."

"I don't get it," I said, "You stand me up and then get pissed. The best defense is a good offense, huh?"

"I don't have a defense. It was just stupidity – jealousy or something, mixed with booze."

"That makes no sense," I said. I didn't bother to remind him of his past behavior. We were still standing in the doorway and I wondered when Dennis would get there.

Enzo looked down at his feet. Those long, dark lashes against his soft face were nearly irresistible. "Anyway, I'm sorry."

"Okay. Fresh start," I said. I stepped inside next to him and let the door close. Dennis was bound to walk up at any second.

"So you wanna go out sometime?"

He'd caught me off guard. I hadn't planned to see him again, never dreamed he'd ask. I couldn't stand there any longer. "Try calling when you're sober."

The door opened and Dennis stepped inside and I moved out of his way. He flashed a grin. Enzo looked at Dennis and looked at me and I thought maybe he saw something between us that would put him off. That's when I realized I still wanted to hear from him.

Enzo turned and started walking slowly toward the counter. Dennis moved closer to me. I didn't give him a chance for any kind of warm greeting. "A little rough out there today."

"No kidding," he said. "It's going to be tough dragging each other onto the boat."

"Even keeping our heads above water."

"I'm surprised they haven't called it off," he said. "I guess they want to get us through so they can start up another class and keep the cash flowing."

I looked at him. He was more cynical than I would have expected. I wondered if he was hoping Enzo could hear.

Dennis grabbed his tanks that were filled and waiting for him beside the door. I saw Enzo looking my way from behind the counter and decided it was a good time to get the Triptone.

"I've gotta get something here," I said. "I'll see you out at the boat."

Dennis looked at me, but I held the door for him and he headed on out.

I went over to Enzo. "I better get some Triptone. I don't want to take any chances."

"Anything you want, sweet."

I didn't say anything, but I had to smile. He said it so soft. He was sexy, no getting around it. I had alarms going off.

He handed over the tablets and I paid and said thanks. I walked over to the water fountain and popped a couple.

"See you in a minute, babe," Enzo called. "Doug's the skipper. I'll be in the water with the class today – keeping an eye on you."

"Okey-dokey," I said. I nodded and went on out. I hoped the ocean was big enough for all of these men that seemed so concerned with my welfare.

The sun stayed behind the clouds, so it was unusually cool and rocky on the way out. I felt fine. I'd brought my shortie wet suit and had it on, half-zipped, to stay warm.

When we anchored for the first dive, Charlie explained the procedure. Instead of each person having a turn to do all the roles, this time the plan was to have one volunteer pretend to be unconscious on the bottom and everybody else take a role in the rescue. He looked around for the volunteer. Nobody said anything, so I put my hand up. What the heck – I didn't mind testing out the mouth-to-mouth and CPR techniques of a few more divers.

On board it was pretty tough to walk without careening sideways. We were arranged in our groups on the benches in the order of getting in, and once we strapped on our tanks we stayed put.

Charlie went in first to lead the group. Dennis and I were last, followed by Enzo. We slipped our fins on and scooted sideways toward the stern. The others were headed down. I stepped off the transom into the cool green. I tilted back, pressed the release button, and let the air escape from my vest immediately so as not to spend any extra time wallowing in the swells on the surface. It was a relief to reach the calm quiet underneath. I heard Dennis hit the water behind me and I dropped down slowly, equalizing my ears. The new regulator worked smooth as a kiss. The whoosh of exhale sounded even and cleansing.

The bubbles from the divers below shimmered past me like jellyfish, gaining speed and size as they came, rushing to their destruction on the surface. I looked over my head and saw Dennis ten feet up and Enzo above him.

Below me, the others were spaced out in a circle waiting. I came down in the middle. As they watched, I touched sand and bent my legs, letting my buttocks come to rest on the bottom, then lay back lightly, limp, but smiling, behind the regulator. It was exciting, pretending to put my life in their hands, like danger under control – they'd fail if I drowned.

Each man had a pre-assigned task in the scenario. I closed my eyes and let diver number one "find" me. It was either the lawyer or the dentist. They looked alike in masks and regulators.

I stayed limp as he looked me over. He reached to my waist and released my weight belt. It dropped on the sand and I watched to make sure somebody picked it up. My rescuer let a small amount of air into my vest, grabbed me under the arms, and started the slow ascent. I saw his eyes and recognized the lawyer. He lifted my shoulders, keeping my head straight to simulate how he would treat an unconscious victim, allowing air to escape gradually from the lungs on ascent.

As we headed slowly upward I held the regulator in my mouth, as instructed, not to risk getting an embolism. There was something stimulating about the nearness of death – just one bubble to the brain was all you needed.

We rose to the surface followed by the whole group. On top the lawyer pushed the button and let enough air into my vest to keep me level. Dennis came forward as diver number two to tow me to the boat. I wondered how he managed to get the mouth-to-mouth position again.

The others bounced in the swells trying to watch. Dennis pushed his mask and snorkel down around his neck and snatched mine off to hand it to another diver, then pulled me up next to his face in position. Water was sloshing over both our heads. I pulled my regulator back out and held my breath, not to take in water, wishing he could get me up a little higher. I exhaled as I saw him coming in for the breath. He put a lock on my lips and puffed. When he left off, I took a gulp of air. A little water slopped in, but I was able to swallow instead of cough. It wasn't a romantic moment like before. Salt stung inside my nose and throat, and I had to time my breaths in between his seals and the waves breaking over my face. There was no way he could control it.

We were making slow progress toward the boat, with him trying to give breaths and swim sidestroke against the four-foot swells and cat's paw breakers. I was taking a breath whenever I got a chance, but there weren't many chances. I couldn't see anybody else or look behind me to know if we were getting close to the boat. All I could see were Dennis's eyes wide, almost in panic, and I wondered how much longer I could keep from pushing him off and grabbing for my regulator to get back into control. I didn't want to mess up the scenario, so I closed my eyes and tried not to hear Dennis huffing and puffing. I concentrated on breathing and counting the waves.

I counted four sets of seven and Dennis let go.

"Got a cramp," he said. He was bent in half reaching for his regulator. "Somebody take over."

I grabbed for my regulator but was jerked under to the side. I was caught halfway though a breath, and some water went down my windpipe. I was being dragged while I choked. I couldn't see without my mask, only bubbles and somebody close. I could feel hands on me, bodies against me. They seemed to be pulling me under more. I couldn't stop choking, couldn't fight my way six inches to the surface. Something was holding me. I reached over my right shoulder, but I couldn't feel the air line, couldn't find my regulator. I was pulled deeper. My chest pounded.

At that second I was released. My head came up and I gasped air before the next wave and coughed and gulped some more. I felt the burn of salt water and stomach acid as I coughed it out. I avoided a swell, gulped more air, coughed again. A wave broke over my head. I struggled hard to cough and gulp without taking in more water.

Enzo came up in front of me wearing his regulator. His dark eyes were open wide. He found my regulator at my side and handed it to me. I felt stupid for not finding it myself. I breathed hard, coughed into the regulator, breathed hard again. He kept staring at me. I felt him grab the neck of my vest. I tried to pull back. I'd had enough of the rescue.

I tried to tell him to let go, but my words were garbled through the regulator and I didn't want to take it out. I tried to push his arm off but he had a solid grip. I gave up and let him level me out. I figured he was showing Dennis what he did wrong. I didn't have a clue what had happened. I closed my eyes and kept breathing on the regulator. He didn't tell me to take it out. I think I would've said no.

When I saw the hull next to me I expected Enzo to let go and the next person to do the lift onto the boat. It looked tough, almost impossible the way the boat was bouncing. They'd have to time the lift just right between the sets of waves. But Enzo didn't let go. He took me to the ladder and began to climb up, hoisting me on his side. I grabbed for the ladder. I wanted to get up myself, get my feet firm on the rungs, finish the rescue another day.

"Quit struggling," Enzo yelled. The crash of waves was so loud I barely heard him even that close to my ear. The stainless steel ladder rose and fell as he tried to climb. "I've got you," he said. I couldn't get a hold even to help, and Enzo had a grip around my waist like an anchor chain.

I pulled the regulator out when my head got far enough up that the waves couldn't get me.

"Enzo," I called. "Let go. I want to climb out myself."

He couldn't hear me or else didn't pay attention. He was still following procedure. I didn't know how he could carry my weight and fight the swells and slippery ladder at the same time, but in a few more seconds he got me out and Charlie grabbed me from above.

Everybody had beat me back to the boat and they were all standing, staring. I didn't see Dennis. I let them pull off my fins and vest. I shivered inside my wet suit, but it was a relief to get the heavy gear off. Charlie half-dragged me to the open area on deck and I closed my eyes, relaxed, and went along with the scenario. He let my head and arms down easy and stepped to the side. His eyes were wide open. I had never seen him so excited. I wondered what happened to Dennis and why the other students weren't getting a turn. Somebody else should be doing the CPR.

Enzo dropped to his knees beside me and pulled the zipper down on my wet suit. He yanked it off my shoulders and pulled it off my arms and down to my waist. It wasn't part of the rescue as I remembered. His face was a rock of concentration. I felt my bikini straps being pulled off my shoulders and I checked to see how much of my top was still on. He'd done a good job of pulling it as far as it could go without stripping me. I could just see the pink edge of one nipple. I felt a cold wind.

He started tugging at the wet suit again and I raised my hips so he could peel it off, all the time thinking that this wasn't part of the rescue and Enzo should have been observing the procedure, not performing it. What happened to the CPR? My bottoms slipped down and they all got a quick flash of the fiery bush. Enzo reached in front of my arms and pulled up my bottoms from the side. He was being more of a gentleman than I would have expected. If I wasn't so fucking cold I could've enjoyed it.

A blanket appeared over my head and Enzo dropped it across my chest, unfolded it, and started tucking it in around me. It wasn't part of the rescue scenario. By then I knew what they were worried about.

"Hey, I'm fine. It's all over," I said. "Where's Dennis?"

"You almost drowned," Enzo said. "You're cold. I don't want you to go into shock."

"I'm a nurse," I said. "I'm fine." I started to sit up and he put his hand right on my chest so I couldn't. "This is ridiculous. I'm fine. If you'd let me put on my dry clothes, I'd get warm in a second."

"No," he said. "You were unconscious."

"Unconscious? When? No way."

"We're doing this by the book," he said. "Relax. I'm not letting you up."

I looked around and saw everybody still staring at me. "This is crazy. I was just going along with the rescue. Let me get up." I started to put more strength into it, tried to move his hand from my chest. "What happened anyway? Somebody was holding me under."

"Lay back," he said. "You're going to wait till we get to the dock. We radioed the paramedics."

"Jesus Christ!" I yelled. That was the last thing I wanted, to be hauled out on a stretcher. I started to push him and he dropped his shoulder on me so I couldn't budge. The anger boiled up in my chest. Then I felt his hand stroke the side of my face and

push my hair back. I gave up fighting it. He was determined to
save me whether I needed it or not. I made myself relax. It wasn't
so bad. I'd get him later for embarrassing me.

"Shh," he said. He was whispering in my ear, softly. "I'm
sorry. We have to do this."

"I'm fine," I said. "I'm all warmed up now. I'm not going to
sue."

He winced and I felt bad. "You could be in shock," he said.
"This is the procedure."

It was useless to argue any more. "Just keep touching my
face," I said. "You're being nice for a change."

He stroked my face again still holding me in place with his
body weight, and I started feeling real soft and warm towards
him, thinking this was the best part of Enzo I'd ever seen. I
watched his mouth and wanted it on mine and wanted his arms
around me and to be somewhere warm. "I'm fine – but you're
sweet," I whispered.

"You know better than that," he said, but it was soft.

When we got to the dock, the paramedics were waiting to
come aboard. They took my vital signs and let me sit up, then
told me I should come to the hospital for observation. I said I was
a nurse and I was already warming up, not going into shock. My
blood pressure and pulse were fine. They were covering themselves, like Enzo and Charlie. I told them the problem had occurred
on the surface, not breathing from the tank, so there was no
reason to suspect an embolism. Finally they accepted my refusal,
but advised me to let somebody drive me home. I said okay,
thinking that when they were gone I would do what I wanted,
which might include having a beer and a sandwich. I was starved.
I still hadn't seen Dennis in all the commotion.

Enzo said he would drive me home and help me get my car
in the morning. I wondered if he continued all this just to get me
into bed. Impossible. Anyway, all he had to do was ask.

Everybody wandered off. Charlie went to finish with the boat.
Enzo told me to stay wrapped up while he rinsed my gear and put
it in his car. I pulled on a T-shirt from my dry-bag and unhooked
my bikini top and slipped the strap off one elbow, then the other,

and pulled the top out of the sleeve. Finally I had dry cloth against my skin.

Dennis came walking over. He sat down on the bench next to me. He shrugged his shoulders and let out air, deflated.

"What happened?" I asked him. "Are you all right?"

"Me?" he said. "What about you?"

"I don't know what the big deal is. I'm fine. All I want to know is what happened."

"Are you sure you're okay? It's my fault. I'm really sorry."

"Fine. What happened?"

"From what I can figure, it was sort of a *Three Stooges* routine. I started it by getting a cramp in my calf, one hell of a cramp. Somehow your regulator line had gotten caught under the knife strapped on my other calf – it was a freak thing – and when I moved back to start massaging my leg, it pulled you under."

"Oh, yeah. I felt myself being pulled down. I couldn't see—"

"Then somebody else – I think it was Charlie – got between us, trying to help, and caught his fin strap on the line and dragged you farther under. He was there splashing and jerking around, taking us both under until Enzo came up from below and unhooked the line. By that time you had already swallowed water and gone unconscious."

"I was never unconscious. I just couldn't get back up."

"I think you were," he said. "Everybody thought so. All of a sudden it was a real rescue. I couldn't do anything besides choke and get myself back to the boat. Enzo took over. He got Charlie to help him."

"I guess they were afraid I'd sue."

"More like they were afraid you'd drown. Then you got so pale and cold. You looked drained."

"It's just the complexion," I said. "It goes to extremes. I'm surprised I wasn't blushing – I felt so stupid."

"No. Stupid is my word for the day."

I turned to see Enzo coming up close. He put his hand on my cheek. The angle of his body blocked Dennis. "You still feel chilly. I better get you home where you can get in bed and warm up."

I felt myself blink when he said "get in bed." I wondered what

Dennis was thinking. It must have been near eighty outside, even
with the heavy cloud cover and breeze, certainly not cold. I wasn't
going to be getting under any covers.

Enzo turned to Dennis. "How's your leg, man?"

"Fine – now. I never had such a bad cramp before."

Enzo looked at Dennis's calves and nodded. "The bigger you
build 'em, the more risk of injury."

"I know," Dennis said. He reached down and rubbed his calf
like it still hurt.

Enzo turned to me. "Ready?"

Dennis was looking at me too, probably waiting to see if I'd
say something about having plans for dinner.

I knew I should say so. I felt a pause.

"Your gear's all rinsed and in my trunk," Enzo said. "Wanna
get going?"

"Yeah, I guess." I looked at Dennis. "I guess I better go home.
Sorry about all the trouble."

"My fault. I'm the one who's sorry."

"Don't worry about it," I said. "I'm just beat. Catch you later.'

17

◆◆◆◆◆◆◆◆◆◆◆◆◆◆◆◆◆

Enzo pulled into a parking space in front of my apartment and went right to the trunk to get my tanks. I tried to help, but he wouldn't let me carry anything. I didn't need to be babied, but what the hell. It was a brand new attitude for Enzo.

I opened the door carefully to check where Ignats and Snickers were hanging out. I wasn't in a mood for a parking lot dash. Snickers was stretched out full length on her back on the couch and Ignats was out of sight.

I closed the door behind Enzo when he brought my gear bag. "You're being awful nice," I said, "but I'm no ninny."

He set the bag on the floor and scooped me up before I knew what was going on. For medium build, he was fucking strong.

"Jesus," I said. I was going to say put me down, but he started nuzzling my tits through the T-shirt and heat shot right through me.

"Ninny," he said. He lifted his head to enjoy the look on my face. "Ninny, ninny." He went to nuzzling and growling. Then he kissed my neck hard, sucking and putting his teeth against my skin. He took any words right out of me.

He'd never been in my apartment before, but he stumbled his way to the bedroom without taking his mouth off my neck, and plopped me on the unmade bed and knelt down next to me. He took my head in close with his hands and held my face, sucking my bottom lip, then working his tongue against mine.

I tried to think what nerve he had, but waves of passion rolled over me and I was wet and empty and weak.

He took his mouth off me and sat on the edge of the bed. His eyes were black and shining. He worked his fingers up under my T-shirt.

"Enzo, Enzo, yes," was all I could whisper. Passion oozed from his name.

He drew the shirt up and dragged his lips across my chest, down my nipples. I gasped with pleasure, a feeling so far from my gasps underwater, yet so near in intensity.

"Warming up?" he asked.

"Uh huh." I stopped thinking of anything. I wanted his weight down on me and his hard cock inside.

"Then it's time for me to go," he said. He pulled my T-shirt down with a jerk.

"What?"

He got up off his knees. His pants bulged above my face. He was huge. I couldn't believe he would leave.

He bent and covered me with the sheet and picked up an orange beeper that had fallen off his belt. "Have to go."

"Not again."

"You need to rest. Get under the covers."

"That's fucking dandy," I told him. My chest was still heaving.

"I have to go. It'll be better next time." He smiled his gleaming grin. "I want you rested." He smoothed back his hair. "You'll see. I'll have you coming like a freight train."

I didn't have anything else to say. I knew it was useless.

He bent down to kiss me.

"Fuck you very much," I said. It came out quiet, without force. "I don't like games."

"You will," he said. "Just wait till we start playing."

He turned and walked.

I lay there tight and hot a long time after he was gone. I put the details of the day together and felt like a real asshole. I pictured Dennis sitting on the bench, watching me take off to be screwed by Enzo – so we both thought! Dennis was too sweet to say anything. I thought about his chiseled arms, his easiness to be with, how we talked.

My vision shifted to Enzo's dark furred chest. I felt a twinge run through me. I knew I was insane. I was electric with Enzo. Enzo with his beeper – no doubt a drug dealer. I'd thought that shit was pretty much over. Hadn't he heard of the "war on drugs"? Okay, it was South Florida. I gave up thinking. I was starved.

I got up to live with myself and made coffee. I picked the mold off six pieces of wholewheat bread, toasted, buttered, jellied, and ate them. I was grating Ignats' yellow squash when the phone rang. It was Charlie. He asked me how I was feeling and I told him great. I told him I'd never been unconscious. There were just a couple hairy moments when I was being jerked around by Dennis's knife strap.

His tone made it clear he didn't believe me and I could feel my nerves shorting out. I wanted to pin his skinny ass to the floor and make him admit they'd all over-reacted. I didn't ever want to hear about "the time Ramona almost drowned."

"I have to go," I told him. "I'm in the middle of feeding my iguana."

"Iguana? How big is he?"

"Big. Thanks for the call. See you in class."

I felt good when I hung up, figuring he'd quit calling after that. I just needed to have some guts to keep things from getting out of control.

The phone rang again. I let the answering machine get it. It was Dennis. He started saying how sorry he was about the accident. I picked up.

"It was a freak thing," I said. "Not your fault. Anyway, I wasn't in any real danger. I just choked on a little water."

"I still feel bad," he said. "Let me take you out and make up for it."

I was glad to see he wasn't going to bring up Enzo. Maybe he hadn't been aware of what was going on after all. Or possibly he was a kind and reasonable man.

He said he planned to go to the gym late the next afternoon

when it wasn't crowded. We could meet there, then grab a sandwich. We had our written test at seven, and afterwards we could celebrate.

I told Dennis I'd like to meet him at the gym, and I told myself I'd just leave Enzo alone. We set the time for four. I decided I'd go early and talk to Rory. I was disgusted with my progress, especially after the diving incident. I knew there was a faster way to build up my strength and I needed that little extra boost. Then I could pour myself into the workouts and see results. I was sure Rory could help me out. I needed to get all those men off my mind and make something of myself.

That afternoon, I was just leaving for the gym when Enzo called, like he knew I was getting ready to dash.

"Sorry. I'm just taking off. Can't talk."

"I save your life and you can't talk to me long enough to set up a date?"

"Hang on, buddy, you didn't save my life."

"You bet your sweet-smelling ass I did."

"Okay, thank you very much. I have to go."

"You're just pissed because I didn't fuck you."

I didn't say anything. I was.

"I wanted to – you know I did. But I had business to take care of."

I looked at my watch. I needed to get going, but I wanted him to know what I felt. "There's no use setting up a date with you. I don't want to sit there waiting for nothing."

"Then I guess I'll see you around."

I was holding an empty connection before I could say anything. Fuck. He knew how to piss me off. I grabbed my gym bag. I'd let him take up my time and still hadn't managed to penetrate his Neanderthal skull.

When I got to the gym there was a guy doing squats, and Rory was squinting over something at the desk. I went ahead to do some bench presses, hoping the guy would leave and I could get Rory into a private conversation before Dennis showed up.

The guy left in the middle of my second set and Rory came

walking over. I wiped the sweat off my chest as I finished out the set. "I don't know how I'll ever get anywhere," I said.

"I felt like that too," he said. "I nearly gave up."

"What kept you going?"

"Wanting to be impressive. The usual, you know."

I looked at him with my softest eyes, trying to draw him out. "A woman."

"But it takes so long. How could you wait? How'd you know she'd still be available?"

He sat down on the bench next to me and looked down on his large hands. "I cut the time down a lot."

"Yeah?" I said. I knew he was deciding whether or not to tell me.

He put his finger in his ear and scratched. "Yeah. I don't do it anymore, but I started on the juice. After I built up I didn't need her – I had plenty of women."

I asked how long it took. He said he gained twenty-five pounds on his first three-month program – all solid muscle. He flexed and smiled.

"Really? You must have spent the whole day working out."

"Three hours a day. It was amazing."

"Yeah. I'll say." I stroked over the puny biceps on my right arm. I imagined myself as a force to be dealt with. "Would I be able to do it that fast?"

"Close," he said. "Women gain fast at the start." He waved his hand toward me. "Your body's not used to the testosterone so it cranks right up. But you have to be careful."

"I know about steroids," I said. "I've seen them used safely for a variety of problems."

"Are you serious about this?" he asked.

"You bet." I pushed my sweaty hair behind my ears and stood up not to miss a word.

He told me it would be expensive, but I could stack Primobolin Depot and Dianabol tabs like he had done, one cc and one tab a day, three times a week max. Primo was a mass builder and Dianabol a fat cutter. He said he'd helped other women build successfully. He would give me a list of foods and an eight-day schedule to follow for my workouts. I should do two sessions of one-and-a-half hours and eat 4,000 lean calories a day for maximum progress.

"Personal training is my specialty. I'll make you a deal."

"Where would I get the drugs?" I asked him. I knew I couldn't ask any of the doctors at the hospital to prescribe them for me.

"Leave that to me. I'll get what you need. Bring the money and I can have the juice in a few days."

I bit my lip before I asked the big question. "How much will it cost?"

He squinted to calculate and I watched his lips figuring. "A three-month supply of the Dianabol – $450, and $900 for the Primo. You should do some B-Complex too, a dollar a shot. I charge $30 an hour – three times a week."

"Whew. It's worse than I thought," I said. "I'll have to see."

I wanted to get started, but it was tough to figure how. I couldn't fit in overtime and workouts. It was hard enough to afford any diving, and the minimum charges for my gear and rescue class were already tough to cover.

"I can get you a month at a time if you want, three month cycle. Pay in thirds. Think about it. I'm not trying to sell you. No extra cash in it for me, just for my time."

I told him I was going to figure it out. I knew I should make some extra money first. But I didn't know how long I could stand to wait. I wanted the strength, the raw power the men could call up so easy. Like Enzo. I wouldn't have needed his help if I'd been strong enough to yank myself away. I'd been held down, without a breath, when all I needed was muscle to set myself free. I wondered what Enzo would think of me as a bodybuilder.

I told Rory I'd talk to him later. I was grunting out a set of squats when Dennis came up behind me in the mirror. His eyes were twinkling. "I see you're all back to normal," he said.

"As normal as I ever was." I set the bar on the posts. I thought I'd feel him out. "In fact," I said, "my whole body seems just the same. I'm not getting anywhere with these weights."

"Takes time. You know. Like anything."

"I can't believe I'll ever get built up like you and Rory." I flexed my pitiful biceps for him to see.

He laughed. "I don't think you want to go that far."

"I'd like the option," I said.

Dennis frowned. He put a warm hand on my shoulder. "Hey, I hope you're not thinking of anything artificial. It's stupid. You know that, being a nurse."

"Yeah. I know. But things can be done sometimes. It's just not an idea you want out to the general public."

"Trust me," he said. "It's not good for you in any way."

"Just like everything I want," I told him.

He put his hand up and lifted my sweaty hair off my back. "Let's talk about something else. Like us."

I twitched. I wasn't ready for "us," but he just wanted to set up details for the evening, after our test. I told him I could go for a beer as long as we went to my place pretty quick so I could get some sleep. I had a day shift I'd swapped for with another nurse. Dennis said we could skip the beer as far as he was concerned.

That night, we both finished the test early. I got up first to have Enzo check my answers. He grunted when he wrote the hundred per cent on top. I laughed. "What did you expect?" I asked.

He didn't answer and I was glad I had a date with Dennis and no games to play. I went out to the car to wait for Dennis to follow me.

We went right to my place and I even didn't look for Ignats or Snickers when I let Dennis in. I led the way into the bedroom and we yanked everything off and hit the bed. Dennis stuck his head between my legs and licked slow and gentle and regular like an animal would cleaning itself, up the inside of my thighs, across my clitoris and back down the other side. He covered the area until I could feel the cool dampness he left by his mouth. He opened my lips and his eyes got soft as he bent and went inside with his tongue. The smell of my female perfume circulated with the ceiling fan, filling the warm room, as I shuddered in waves.

He crawled across my body and laid himself between my thighs and I could see the gloss of my juices and his saliva on his

chin. He covered my mouth with his and I tasted the ocean from
my own source. It took me farther into my senses, the world of
taste and smell and touch, where there was no thinking, only
reaction. He slid inside me and my whole feeling concentrated
into that small pocket. I felt myself bearing down against his
weight, and the opposites coming together, hard and soft, in and
out, him and me, in perfect balance till we collapsed together.

I heard regular breathing and opened my eyes to look at
Dennis. He was shiny and beautiful in the light filtering through
the ficus leaves. The moon must have been full.

I propped myself on my elbow and gazed down his classic
tapered torso to his abdomen. I bent to kiss the shadowy hollows
under his ribs. He didn't move. I looked closer. There was a thick
black hair on his left hip that didn't fit his sleek hairless skin. It
was too black, too dark, too long, too wavy. It was Enzo's. An
Enzo hair was trying to come between us, as if Enzo and I had
done anything. It had hidden itself, waiting to make its appearance
by moonlight.

It struck me – how unfair. Then I realized it was only Enzo's
sudden appointment that kept me off him. I would have straddled
him in a second, taken whatever I could get. I still would. I had
no sense at all.

I put my fingers together and slowly, delicately, lowered my
hand to pick off the hair.

I didn't get it. It was plastered to him with sweat. He didn't
move. I tried again. He raised his head. I made a dive for his
mouth and at the same time wiped from his hip outward onto the
sheet. I did it again, just to make sure. I was caressing his face
with my left hand, kissing his cheeks, forehead, ears, brushing the
sheet with my right hand until I felt sure the hair was gone. I
lifted my face and looked into Dennis's eyes, smiled, kissed his
lips light. My head was drifting with Enzo still in there.

"You're sweet," Dennis said.

"Not me," I told him. "You're way off."

He kept nodding to disagree. I dropped my head on the
pillow. He was sweet enough to think everybody else was.

Dennis fell back asleep and I lay there. It was one of those nights with high humidity and no breeze. His extra body heat raised the temperature of the room. I started thinking of Enzo again, wondering what he wanted from me anyway, thinking he'd left that hair on purpose for Dennis, a ridiculous thought.

I got up to look for Ignats, making a little noise getting from bed to floor. I looked at Dennis, hoping he might wake up and leave, so I wouldn't have to throw him out to sleep, but he didn't move.

I turned on the table lamp in the living room. Snickers was curled on the couch in one of her normal spots. I got down and looked under it, no Ignats. I checked under the dining room table, on all the chairs, the kitchen, behind the refrigerator. I checked the bathtub, no Ignats; thank God, no pearly python. The memory made me shiver. I sat down for a pee. I wondered if Claire had gotten over Spike.

I decided Ignats was probably under the bed, under sleeping Dennis. I took some monkey biscuit and squash in to see if I could find that beady-eyed reptile. I wondered if those yellow eyes glowed in the moonlight – I thought of Enzo's dark shining eyes.

I got down on the floor and looked under the bed. Ignats was in the far corner. He'd probably been listening to our fucking, getting his mating behaviors stirred up in that primitive brain of his.

I put the dish near his head and watched while he did nothing. I scooted backwards.

Dennis's face was square in front of me as I pulled my head out. "Who's under the bed?"

"Just a little friend of mine."

"Not Enzo, is it?" he asked.

I felt myself jerk.

He laughed. "You said little."

"It's my lizard, silly."

"Then I'm not far off."

I made a mouth and shook my head. I was tempted to admit he wasn't. I wondered why Dennis was on Enzo's case. Maybe he'd been talking to Charlie.

I kissed him. "I have to get up early," I said.

"Yeah. I need to get going."

I bent down and started picking up his clothes, dropping them in front of him on the bed. I knew it would be smart to latch on to Dennis. The sex was great and the conversation good, comfortable. Besides his looks, he was polite, honest, gentle, not pushy or controlling – a man who liked women. He had goals toward a fulfilling future. There could only be a few men alive to compete with all that – but something in me didn't care, and my brain couldn't change it.

18

◆◆◆◆◆◆◆◆◆◆◆◆◆◆◆◆

All we had left of the class was the night dive. It was scheduled for Saturday, followed by a big party at the lawyer's house on the Intracoastal. He'd promised catered food and champagne.

I didn't hear from Charlie or Enzo during the week. I wondered if they'd both given up on me. I knew it would be for the best – with Enzo especially. He was just bad news wearing pants. I kept telling myself that.

I met Dennis at the gym a few times during the week, but I told him I couldn't get together afterwards. I enjoyed his company, but I was afraid of starting a habit. I just didn't have that helpless-in-love feeling that closes off thinking about anything else.

Saturday was calm and clear, great conditions for the night dive. I packed all my gear and a thin cotton dress, underwear I could decide whether to wear or not later.

We had a briefing in the classroom before the dive and Charlie explained that he had a special mission for us. It wasn't exactly on the lesson plan, but he thought it would be good experience. He was obviously trying to impress us with his seriousness. We looked at each other waiting for him to get to the point.

"We're going to take a blind diver down tonight," he said finally.

It sounded crazy to me. The thrill of diving at night lay mostly

in seeing the night creatures – and feeling that undetected pred-
ators were lurking a few feet away, scenting you out and deciding
if you were tasty. That sounded close to a normal day for a blind
person. Why go underwater at night? It was overkill.

"Steve is his name. He'll be here in a few minutes. He's com-
pleted his Open Water Certification. He knows what he's doing."

I figured maybe the dark helped him feel equal – or macho. I
couldn't blame him. If I went blind, I'd skydive naked or something. I made a mental note to do it. Everybody would help you
out and give you plenty of leeway for your actions, like we were
ready to do with this Steve.

I caught the end of Charlie's little talk. Half the group would
go with Steve for the first dive and the other half the second.
Charlie would supervise Dennis, the lawyer, the dentist, and me.
I wondered what Enzo was up to.

I saw Steve already on board when I went to the car to get
my gear. I wondered who dropped him and left. He was just sitting
there.

I was first at the boat. Steve heard my steps on the asphalt.
He stood up tall and leaned forward. "Hey there, let's go diving."
He said it just loud enough to hear, sort of like a come on. I
wondered if he could tell I was female from my walk.

"Hi," I said. "I'm Ramona."

"Steve," he said. I couldn't see anything unusual about his
light blue eyes, except they weren't aimed at my chest. He had
long brown hair in a ponytail, and freckles, and an earring. He
was wearing a dark blue-black, tie-dyed shirt and cut offs – a
blind hippie diver, odd combination.

"Won't be long now," I said. I set my stuff down and went
for my tanks. "Be right back."

I passed Dennis and winked. He puckered his lips and kissed
air. Charlie walked by and I wondered if he'd caught our signals.
I glanced at his trim gluteals.

Dentist Bob had brought two catered trays of hors d'oeuvre
for a snack. When the boat got underway he opened it all up on
one of the benches. There were crackers and chips and dips,
cheeses, shrimp, and deviled crabs.

Steve walked right toward the bench. "I smell food," he said.

I was standing to the side, admiring the spread, waiting for Bob with the paper plates.

The deck lurched. Steve took an extra step. I grabbed his arm. "Hold it," I said. "No cutting in line."

He held my shoulder and regained his balance. He laughed. His hand slipped down over my left breast and stopped at my waist to hold on. I could see he'd honed his survival skills. I wondered if he'd faked the stumble. But did he know I was standing there?

I looked into those blue eyes. They were opaque.

Bob brought the plates and handed me one. "Start any time," he said.

I looked around. Nobody seemed to have noticed Steve's feel. The lawyer reached for a shrimp.

"Want me to fix you a plate?" I asked Steve.

"Sure. You can feed me if you like," he said.

I gave him a wise-guy look, never mind he couldn't see it. "Okay," I laughed. "What would you like?"

"Oooh. My kind of girl."

I looked around to see if Enzo or Dennis or Charlie were watching this conversation. Dennis was busy with his gear and the other two must have gone up top.

"What smells so good?" Steve asked. His nose was practically in my hair.

"The deviled crabs," I told him.

"I doubt it," he said. His hand came up to my pony tail, and rested on the back of my neck, his fingers massaging lightly. "Same hair-stylist."

"Yeah, it's handy for diving," I said. "This is your last chance. What do you really want? Crabs, shrimp, cheese?"

"You keep asking, and I'll tell you."

I wondered if he could feel the goosebumps he was putting on my neck or if he was always so bold. Yeah, he got a lot of leeway.

Dennis came walking up and introduced himself to Steve and asked if he'd been on a night dive before. I got a plate and put a

couple crabs and shrimp and crackers on it and handed it to Steve.
I went back for my own.

I was scooping some dip onto my plate when I felt a hand on
my hip. Steve had great aim.

"Thanks," he said. His lips were so close to my ear his breath
tickled. "See you soon, sweet."

I wondered if he picked words with s's on purpose. He'd said,
"See you," just like anybody, but he didn't leave.

Enzo stepped up, glaring. "Let's get your gear ready, Steve,"
he said.

"Going down soon, baby," Steve said. He gave a wink in my
direction. He was full of surprises.

The six of us went off the platform in order, with Steve in the
middle. He was wearing a dive mask like everybody else. He didn't
have a problem knowing which way was down.

We landed at sixty feet. It was a high reef with lots of grunts
and snappers swarming along the jagged edges, playing their food-
chain games. We were supposed to give Steve a tour somehow, so
we headed down the reef against the current. All of us but Steve
had our lights focused on the reef, checking the holes for lobster
and morays. You couldn't see anything outside of those small
flashlight beams and foggy green glows of the cyalumes attached
to our tanks.

I stopped next to a rock with a sleeping parrot fish beside it.
Dennis saw what I was doing and took Steve's hand. I saw Steve
jerk until he realized it was one of us. Then he reached out.
Neither of us was wearing gloves and I guided his hand slowly
toward the fish. I put his fingers lightly on the smooth area below
the dorsal fin. He must not have known what it was, but he didn't
try to move away, just stroked the fish like he was reading Braille,
until it woke up and moved off. I figured I'd describe it all later.
He turned his head toward my bubbles and reached right into my
BC onto my breasts. He couldn't really feel anything through the
thick latex of the wet suit, but it was a bold move. He knew
nobody could see and I couldn't say anything. I took his hand out
and placed it at his side. He was damn capable of finding his way
around in the dark. He could rival Enzo for nerve.

I felt fingers tug on the edge of my shortie bottoms. Dennis and Charlie were with Steve. I knew it wasn't the dentist or lawyer. I didn't turn around. I reached behind me and felt my hand pressed against nylon fabric – speedos. Ha! Think of the devil – Enzo. He must have been wandering by himself. He rubbed my hand across his suit.

"Ouch," I yelled through my regulator. He had a sea cucumber inside there, hard and scratchy through the nylon, over a foot long. I laughed as I exhaled. I wondered if he took it to mean we were on friendly terms. I guess we were.

Everybody helped drag Steve along when it was time to head up. He had no concerns.

We all shook hands on the dock. Charlie and Enzo congratulated Dennis and me. We split up to head for our cars. I told Dennis I'd catch him at the party and took my time rinsing my gear so I could arrive alone. I wanted to be one of the group, not half of a couple.

When I pulled in at the party I saw Enzo's, Dennis's and Charlie's cars lined up on the street. It was going to be interesting. I pulled in front of Enzo.

I grabbed my dry bag and my purse and headed to the door. The lawyer, Rick, opened it and I could hear the others out back, but I asked him to show me a bathroom where I could dry off and change. He told me to feel free to take a shower.

I got into the firm spray and soaped up, enjoying the hot water and the flowery scent of the rose-carved soap that he'd laid out with a towel and washcloth. It always felt great to get the dry salt off and warm up.

I had the water on strong but I thought I heard someone at the door. I hadn't thought to lock it, but surely anybody could hear the shower running. They must have had plenty other bathrooms in that house. I saw movement through the shower door and opened it. Steve was moving slowly into the room with his arms outstretched.

I started to say something, but then remembered he couldn't see me anyway. I figured he didn't have any idea who was in there. Maybe he was lost.

"Ramona," he called.

"Steve?" I watched him close the door.

"Can I come in with you?" He was walking toward me across the tile.

"What?" I couldn't believe what I was hearing.

He stripped off his shirt. "I thought you might help me find my way around this bathroom."

"No. I don't think so," I said.

He stopped undressing and looked toward me, only his eyes were focused above my head. "They told me you're a nurse, honey. I need a little nursing." He unhooked his belt and his jeans slid down and his buckle clanked on the tile. No underwear and he was hard.

"Get the fuck out of here," I said. I was glaring at him and he was looking a little to my left.

He stepped gracefully out of his pantslegs and walked slowly toward the shower.

I put out my arm to stop him before he reached the stall. He was a couple inches shorter than I was and small built, but strong. I tried to close the door with my other hand, but he lunged and caught hold of it. He realized what he had and pulled it away from me and stepped inside. I was stunned by my lack of strength.

The water was hard on his face but he didn't even blink. I thought of yelling, but I didn't want everybody running in there to help me.

He got his face into my chest. My breasts were all soapy and he started smearing himself around. He was wallowing on me until I managed to pry him off by pushing the side of his head. His hand came up between my legs. I couldn't hit him, he was too pathetic. I twisted his arm away and held it to his side. He didn't try to force it back.

I kept shaking my head. It was so ridiculous.

His other hand made its way down to his penis. It was out straight and stiff, nearly touching my thigh. He put his foot on the wall and grabbed himself, pumping hard, his head bobbing in rhythm.

He pumped and pumped while I stood there in some kind of

dream. I felt like a voyeur watching the expression on his face. Anybody would say he was taking advantage of me, but it didn't feel that way. He was too desperate to care what happened. He came and I watched the spurts. The come flowed down his hand and mixed with the suds in his pubic hair. I wondered if he knew what his come looked like. I let his hand go. He slumped against the wall to get his breath.

I felt awkward in the silence. "I never saw anybody do that before," I said.

He looked up at my face. "I've never seen myself – blind since birth. It was an oxygen problem in the incubator. I was a premie."

"I've heard of that," I said. There I was being sucked into a conversation. I couldn't believe it. "Christ, I should call the police on you."

He stepped closer, put one arm on each side of me against the shower stall door and wall. "I'll suck your toes to make up for it." He didn't say anything else, just stood looking with his blank eyes.

"You're a real pervert," I said. I tried to sound disgusted.

"Better a pervert than a charity case. Don't you think?"

"That's one way of looking at it," I said.

"It's the rep I'm working on."

"Well, keep my name out of it if you don't want trouble booking your next dive. Okay?"

"No problem, babe."

Steve was the coolest sucker I'd ever run across. I knew I should do something about him, but I didn't have the heart. I leaned my head back and let the water flow down my face and chest, expecting him to edge on out.

He stepped forward and rinsed himself and rubbed his eyes. I watched. He reached down and gave his penis a few swipes and reached under his balls.

"Mind if I take a piss?" he asked.

"Jesus. I can't believe you're asking."

"I'm not rude."

I opened the door and stepped out onto the mat and grabbed

my towel. He held his penis and I watched the full steady stream.
Men and their dicks. Incredible. I gave up.

When he was finished I turned off the water for him. He felt
his way out and I took the towel from the bar and put it against his
chest. He said thanks and went to drying his balls.

I ignored him and dried, and put my beach dress on, and got
out my brush.

"Be seeing you, Ramona. It was great."

I just stared, thinking that he hadn't seen me and never would.
He was all dressed and had his hair combed back.

"See you," I said.

He found the doorknob and made his way out. I hoped
nobody was standing in the hall, waiting to get in. I didn't want
to think about it.

I finished brushing my hair and took my wet bathing suit to
the car without running into anyone. I headed out back where the
music was. A lot of the guys had brought wives or dates, and there
were men I didn't recognize, probably Rick's friends. I slipped past
the groups of people talking and headed toward a big cooler
by the pool. I reached in and got an icy beer and took it to sit on
the edge and dangle my feet. I thought I'd wait for people to come
over to me.

It was only a minute till Charlie showed up. He sipped on a
can of Bud and stared into the swimming pool. His blond hair
was wild, and the flickering pool light on his face made him look
demonic. The demon from the depths, hardly. I felt my body
softening with the beer and the feel of warm water. I looked
around for Dennis or Enzo and didn't see them.

I motioned Charlie to sit next to me. "Did we do okay
tonight?" I asked him.

He looked up and winked. "Just fine," he said. "We'll have a
little ceremony later. I'll give you your signed certification form.
You brought a picture?"

"Sure," I said.

I looked at his impish face and compact muscular frame. Van
Morrison's "Moondance" came over the speakers and picked up

the rhythm of the flickering water. I had that feeling of being in a movie.

Charlie pointed at the pool. "Get your clothes off," he said. "I want to see fire under water."

I knew he must be fairly drunk already, to be that bold and referring to my pubic hair, but I couldn't resist. Maybe the incident with Steve put me up for a dare. "Encourage me," I said.

He started to pull off his shirt. I looked around and everybody was over on the patio drinking and talking. I was in shadow under a tree. I put my purse on a chair, kicked off my shoes, and grabbed the top of my dress. I looked straight at Charlie and then yanked it over my head. I looked around. Nobody else was watching. I dropped the dress on the chattahoochee and bent down to pull off my panties. I stepped out of those and plunged right into the water. It was like a bath.

I looked up and saw Charlie naked and froglike on the edge. He dove in with a clean cut. His moving shadow curved behind me and next thing I felt was a hard-on coming up between my legs from the back. Charlie? The heat moved right up to my neck. I turned my head to look at his face over my shoulder. His blond hair was doused forward and his eyelashes glistened. He was grinning, licking at the cascade of water running down his face.

I heard a splash on the other side and turned.

Enzo stood next to me. He whipped his head side to side to shake the water from his long dark hair. He smoothed it straight back and jerked his chin toward me.

"What's up?" he said.

I felt my eyes open wide. I caught myself from looking down, but he must've figured what was there anyway, seeing how Charlie backed away from my hips.

"Always something," I said. I grinned. It was almost too funny to let go. I looked into the water and saw Enzo had his suit on. Charlie moved to my right, out of Enzo's line of vision.

"No bathing suits allowed in the pool," I told Enzo.

"No problem." He slipped the speedos down and stepped out of them. I watched his body under water, but I couldn't see much.

I felt movement in the water as Charlie passed me headed for the steps. He was putting some space between himself and Enzo.

I heard a crunch of footsteps and looked up. Dennis came walking across the chattahoochee with a beer in one hand and Steve on his other elbow. Steve's lanky body slumped loose and bony next to Dennis's strong, sculpted shape. I remembered that Steve had more strength in those pitiful arms than I had in mine.

Dennis looked down into the pool. "Having fun, guys?"

"Sure," I said. "Want to join us?"

Dennis looked at each of us. He looked back at me. "Too many dicks in one pool."

"Always room for one more," I said. I laughed. He sounded pissed and I wanted him to get over it and get in. I glanced at Enzo. He had his arms crossed, staring up at Dennis. Charlie had moved against the wall. He was fishing for a cigarette out of his shirt pocket.

"Hey, I'm game," Steve hollered. "Lead me to the steps, Dennis."

Dennis didn't move. "Ramona, I'm cutting out of here in a few minutes. You planning to come?"

It was an ultimatum. I wasn't surprised. "It's early," I said. "We haven't got our certificates yet."

"Charlie'll hold them at the shop, won't you?"

Charlie exhaled smoke through his nose. "Yeah. If you want." He was looking at me, frowning, his elbow bent on the concrete edge with the cigarette pointed away, cool as a billboard ad.

Enzo was still standing in front of me with his arms crossed, his legs seeming wide apart.

I imagined his cock hard under the surface. I didn't want to make a decision.

He looked up and down between me and Dennis.

"What's doing?" Steve said. He let go of Dennis and started feeling forward with his foot. "I can smell my way to the chlorine, but it'd be nice to have a hand down the steps."

I turned to the steps automatically – maybe it was my nurse's training. I didn't mean it as a yes to Dennis, but he picked up my dress and held it toward me.

I put my foot on the first step as I shook my head no. Enzo stepped up and put a hand on my biceps. Before I knew what he was doing, he reached his other arm behind my opposite shoulder and then slipped the hand down under the backs of my knees. He pulled me against his chest and I was slung half over his shoulder. I could feel the cool breeze on my back right down to my labia resting on his forearm. He trudged up the steps.

"Enzo! Stop!" I yelled.

"You're going with me – straight out the front door."

"No way. Put me down." He had me in a tight one-man carry. I started to pull on the fingers that were clamped to my thighs. He was making easy progress up the steps. I looked behind me to see Charlie still by the wall lighting up. Dennis was glaring down with a hand on his hip still holding my dress. Steve was like a statue, holding the air, sensing something.

Enzo grabbed my ponytail that was flying in his face and pulled it back. He knew he had me under control.

"What do you want, babe? Say what you want. I think you want to go home with me."

I looked sideways into those shining black eyes. He was asking, not telling, and his hard muscles and soft skin were powerful motivation. I was hot against him, sharing his heat. I was nodding yes. "You're insane," I said. "You're terrible."

I pointed to my dress in Dennis's hand, and my purse on the chair. We were out of the pool and I expected him to set me down, but he grabbed the purse and Dennis handed the dress to him, shaking his head. It was more coordinated than any of our dive scenarios. Enzo didn't even stop moving. He left his trunks where he'd dropped them.

The whole party got a lingering shot of the fiery bush from underneath as we flashed by. By then I was going with it, feeling the breeze. Enzo pushed past a crowded food table and walked down the path and through the kitchen door as a woman stepped out. Her mouth was open at our dripping nudity. I wondered if Enzo had a hard on. I didn't care. I stared back. I wouldn't be seeing most of those people again. Let them think I was drunk. It was my grand finale. I only hated the thought of Dennis, how nice he was.

Enzo set me down by the passenger side of his car and put my dress and purse into my hands. I looked around to see if anybody was watching, not caring if they were. Enzo put his face down to mine and his arms around my back and gave me a long, sweet kiss. I felt my body fire up in waves and I put my hands on his long hair in back and held him and wondered what craziness was happening.

"I didn't want you going home with Dennis," Enzo said. "There wasn't much time."

"Why the hell such a dramatic exit?" I said.

"I know you. You're an exhibitionist."

I crossed my naked arms and shook my head.

He slid his eyes down me in one of his lazy glances and then opened his car door.

"I have my car," I said.

"I'll follow you home." He shut the door and walked around to the driver's side, naked and uncaring.

I looked around. I set the purse on the hood of his car and wiggled my dress over my head and shoulders and pulled it down on my hips. I took my purse and walked across the drive to my car. I was shaking my head in awe at myself, but I felt a grin on my face.

I watched his lights flash on and got in and started up. I knew I shouldn't have let Enzo get away with his scene, whether I liked it or not. When I turned the key I had an odd feeling that I'd just started up something besides the engine in my old Datsun. I knew it was a bad idea. I put in the clutch and hit the gas.

Enzo was still naked, not even carrying a towel, when he closed the car door and strode up to me at my door. I didn't look around for neighbors.

He scooped me up and carried me inside all the way to my bed, a repeat of the rescue scenario. At least he had nowhere to carry his beeper. If he tried to leave this time, I'd kill him.

He didn't put me down. He had me in his arms lengthways

and he peeled my dress to the waist with one hand and nuzzled my tits, sucking and rubbing and growling. His mouth was all over me hard, and I gasped with the surges running through me. He kept it up until I was dying to get my mouth on his and smear the rest of me along his sweating naked length. He held me hard as I writhed.

He lowered me, then dropped me the last foot onto the bed. His mouth closed over mine and his cock slipped inside me. It was as big and hard as I knew it must be. I raised my hips and pushed myself against him, farther into the feeling.

He took his mouth off and all I could do was breathe his name, "Enzo, Enzo" – how could he be named so perfect? The sound blended with the humidity and hung there all around me.

He put a finger to his lips and I thought he was trying to motion me to be to be quiet, but he wet it and I felt him working it into my sphincter, massaging inward, slowly, while he worked me in rhythm with his cock. I was packed so tight I couldn't feel the separate sensations. From the hips down I was like one working machine of pleasure. The waves were building their way through my body, like electric currents meeting between my pelvic bones. I shuddered and rolled side to side, almost forever, until I finally collapsed.

When he felt me relax he pulled out slowly, first finger then penis. I closed my eyes. Then I felt him below me. He turned me on my stomach and pulled me down the sheets so my legs were hanging off the side, my feet touching the floor and him squatting between. He opened me up with his hands, got his hot, wet tongue inside my buttocks. I heard him take a breath through his nose and felt the warm exhalation. He held me by the hips while his tongue settled into juicy stroking, and I looked back to see his black eyes glazed above my cheeks. I gave myself up to the sound of surf in my ears, and the surges running through my body. If that's what he liked, it was fine with me.

He pulled out for a second and put fingers to his mouth. He moved the hand down below the level of the bed, but I could see from the jerk of his arm what he had a hold on and how hard he was yanking at it. He started to tense up and I thought he was

going to come, but he crawled back onto the bed and I raised my
buttocks to meet his cock and he slipped into my pussy, and I
went mindless again, bearing down, and bearing down harder. He
started to moan and I joined in and kept coming in a haze of little
explosions till he stopped moving.

He fell to my side and settled against me like a spoon and
pushed a pillow under my head. The fingers of his left hand came
up between my buttocks and stayed snug between the halves, and
he put his right arm across my ribs, his hand on my left breast. I
could smell the tangy scent of myself on his fingers. We were
wrapped in our hot musky atmosphere.

I drifted off, knowing now why I wanted Enzo, not worrying
what trouble it might cause if I were to fall in love with an
asshole . . . or what trouble he might be in for . . . if he'd fallen in
love with mine.

19

◆◆◆◆◆◆◆◆◆◆◆◆◆◆◆◆

Charlie mailed my certificate, along with a note that said, "Congrats." I knew I wouldn't be hearing from him again. That was good. I felt a little sorry about Dennis, but there'd been something missing between us that I couldn't define. I only knew Enzo had it. It was something I couldn't stay away from.

Since the diving class ended I had more time. I pretty much filled it with Enzo, thinking of him, when I wasn't visiting. It was like I'd been swept out by a powerful riptide. Was it the challenge? Love? I kept bucking, but losing ground every second. It was a workout for my soul.

I started going to the gym at hours when Dennis was unlikely to be there. I took the ten hours at thirty dollars an hour with Rory as my personal trainer. He told me after that I'd be able to manage my own workouts. He'd be glad to spot for me if I came in when he was working. I wondered if he planned on having something more than a professional relationship. I didn't bother to think about it.

He told me it would be six months of hard work before I could see much toning unless I got the "roids," as he called them. If I put myself on a rigid training schedule, I could only put on five pounds of lean muscle mass in a year. It sounded like an awful lot of time for so little. I knew I was going to have to find a way to get the money I needed. I was thinking about a cash advance on another credit card.

I'd taken graveyard shift so I had my days free if I didn't spend the whole time sleeping. I was seeing Enzo off and on in the early evenings when he didn't have to teach. He seemed to enjoy it, but he didn't make a point of inviting me. I'd call and if he was home, he'd say, "Sure, come on over." It was like his mind was filled with other things, but he was happy when I made the suggestion. Sometimes I intended to wait for an invitation but lacked the willpower. I had hot cravings for him, just picturing his soft neck. That strength of feeling scared me. I didn't want to lose my freedom so soon. But he could slather on the charm, and I was having fun. When I wanted out it should be easy, just stop inviting myself.

One evening before my shift I was headed over to his house. I realized we'd been seeing each other a few times a week for over a month. We hadn't talked about anything but diving in that time, and it was a little strange how we got on with mostly body language. I didn't know anything about him or how he felt about me. There was no movement toward intimacy.

I told myself that was what I wanted, I just needed to get on with my own life and goals. I hadn't been diving since the class and I wasn't making any noticeable progress in the gym. I wondered what Enzo would think of me starting on the steroids. He'd probably like to see me built up. I thought I could open up a conversation about it, if nothing else.

He'd said he was cooking dinner that night. I couldn't imagine it, but I was happy to eat anything somebody else cooked. I especially liked the idea that Enzo was cooking for me.

I smelled garlic when I parked my car in his driveway. I opened the front door and breathed in the sharp aroma. "Mmm," I said.

Enzo stuck his head out from the kitchen, then walked out drying his hands on a towel until he stopped and wrapped his arms around my shoulders.

I could feel the strength in his muscles. He had a lot in reserve.

"Mmm, mmm," he said. He nuzzled my neck, started the chills working. He liked to see me dazed.

I moved my head around until I got his lips and I pushed my tongue in and let myself float on a wave of heat until he pulled back and looked into my eyes.

"Hungry?"

"Starved."

"Me too." He put his hot mouth back on my neck and I felt his hands pulling up my uniform, stretching my panties aside. He got a finger in me. "Mmm," he said. "Let's eat."

I didn't know whether to head toward the kitchen or the bedroom. He had his games. He didn't make a move except for the finger. It roved upward between my buttocks. I made myself relax as he stroked gently toward the inside of my sphincter. Finally he pulled his finger out and led me toward the kitchen. I saw him take a whiff of his knuckle before he washed his hands. I figured the washing was only for my benefit. He picked up a fork and fished in the pot for a piece of pasta.

"It's ready," he said.

"You're strange."

"I know. There's nobody as good as me."

He drained the angel hair and tossed it with garlic and oil. Broccoli and grated white cheese were in bowls on the counter. He opened the oven and pulled out a loaf of bread wrapped in foil.

I sat down and salivated. Enzo had a few pretty good tricks.

He dished out a mound of soft pasta shining with the olive oil and garlic, placed two bright green broccoli stalks on top, ripped off a piece of steaming bread, and dropped it on my plate. He lit a candle and poured us each a glass of Chianti. "To decadence," he said. We clinked and sipped.

I focused on his lips so full and soft on that glass. He wasn't the Enzo I'd thought.

He twirled huge mouthfuls of spaghetti and slurped them into his mouth. His lips shone with oil. He had a beautiful chiseled face and his eyes were deep black by candlelight, hair waved back softly. It was a face to gaze on between your breasts and legs.

I twirled a fork of pasta against my spoon. I don't know how long I kept twirling.

"I know you're not Italian with that red hair," he said. "Besides, a real Italian doesn't use a spoon. So, how'd you get the last name Romano?" He took a gulp of the Chianti and swallowed.

"You're right," I said. "My mother picked the name. She says it's poetic. She isn't normal."

"And you are?"

"What do you mean?" I asked. I couldn't tell if he was teasing or not.

"Not a thing, sweetheart." He stuck another clump of angel hair in his mouth and crossed his eyes at me.

"I used to like the idea of her picking a name she liked – I thought she was going against the rules. Then I found out it was a trick to keep a man, convince him he was my father. Orazzio Romano. It was a good try, but he didn't buy it." I took a long drink of wine. "It turned out better anyway. She'd have done anything he said to keep him."

"Hmm," Enzo said. He was chewing, his eyes drifting. I wondered if he was really listening.

I shrugged. "I've been thinking of getting more serious about my weight training. Start to work towards a goal – build up and then get seriously into diving, as a profession."

"Oh, yeah?" He put his hand on my thigh and squeezed it, like he was choosing a roast beef. "Pretty solid already," he said.

I was sitting next to him and slipped my garlicky tongue into his ear. Ears and garlic. It was a good combination. "What do you think? I want to build my upper body to improve my strength. I've got a trainer down at the gym."

Enzo opened his eyes. "Sure. You can do that. But it's time-consuming."

I nibbled his lobe and worked down his neck a little. "I know. I'm trying to figure out how I can manage it. It's expensive."

"Good luck," he said. "I started once, but I couldn't keep up with it." He chewed the crust off a thick slice of garlic bread and took another swig of Chianti. He looked at my face with pleasure in his eyes. It was the same look as when he'd sniffed his knuckle. He enjoyed me with all his senses.

"What I was thinking is trying a few weeks of steroids."

"That'd work."

"You think so?"

He looked me over. "Yeah. I'd like to see you a raging, fucking female bodybuilder."

"Think you could handle me?"

He laughed. "Without even trying." He picked up my arm and squeezed the biceps. He just looked at me, like my puniness was self-evident.

"I'm gonna give it a try," I said. "What the heck – it'll be worth it just to show you."

"Hey, I'll be your backer. I'd like to contribute to this project."

I felt my eyes light up. It wasn't even the money, for the most part. Now I felt Enzo had some interest in me – it was some kind of commitment. I'd told myself I didn't want anything like that, but I couldn't deny the warm feeling. I kissed him hard. "I could use a little help – I'll pay you back, promise."

By the time we finished eating there was only forty-five minutes before I had to leave for my shift. He said it was time to finish what he started. He threw me over his shoulder and took me in to the bed.

That night I was late for the first time at the hospital. It was only twenty minutes, but it scared me – the influence Enzo had.

At least the night was quiet. Just a guy with acid splashed in one eye, one case of anaphalactic shock caused by ant bites, and a broken toe. We never had a rush, nobody bleeding or begging for fast service, a rare night. When I went to the drug cabinet I glanced at the labels I wasn't familiar with. I knew there was no Winstrol or Primobolin Depot, but I had it on my mind. I was desperate to get started. Now I wanted to impress Enzo too.

20

I went home that morning and had dreams about pills falling off shining metal shelves and shards of glass bouncing off my forehead barely missing my eyes. I woke up during a storm and thought it was true, and that I'd lost my job.

I knew it was caused by anxiety. I felt out of control, fearful of getting caught using steroids. But that was silly, nobody would know. It really wasn't anyone's business, as long as I wasn't a hazard on the job. I needed to put some weight on my bones, solid weight, to become an A-1 diver. I wanted to be able to save myself or anybody – carry Enzo naked across the lawn.

I slept until four in the afternoon and woke up feeling tired and sweaty. I dragged myself into the living room and sat on the couch, looked around for Ignats. Snickers had tucked herself up like a tiny package on the bookcase.

Enzo had business to take care of that night so I didn't plan to see him. I had to do laundry – no clean uniforms left – and wanted to get some details from Rory and work out.

I saw the tip of Ignats' tail at the opposite end of the couch. He was always stuck in the same spot. I wondered why he didn't get tired of facing that corner. He'd been eating regularly from his dish, but spent most of his time in the same territory. I wondered if Snickers had him bamboozled.

I got down on the floor and took a look at him. He was

awake, posing strong and silent. His body was close and I put my hand under the couch and moved it slowly towards him along the carpet. Magda's critter had been docile and cheerful to be handled, but not Ignats. I hadn't tried to pick him up lately. I just wanted to hold him for a minute.

As my hand got near his shoulder I could see his eyes following. He reminded me of Enzo. I saw something coldly sexual in his gaze. His body was perpendicular to my arm and I slid my fingers over his back, not to frighten him, and grasped his midsection underneath, sort of scooping him up with my wrist and forearm and pulling him towards me. I loved the texture of his skin, the thin, tiny beaded green canvas that was his external protection. He had such strength and agility.

He didn't lurch but I could see the muscles in his limbs flex. I gradually scooted him closer, until I could bring him out from under the couch. I put him gently against my body and rocked back and got to my knees. He was still steady, but his eyes darted at random from me to various points in the room. I let the pressure off with my fingers and waited with him lying on my arm across my chest. He looked up at my face and I could tell the need for freedom was penetrating his reptile brain and soon he would take a leap.

I held still and in a few seconds his claws began to bite into my forearm and he crossed to my opposite shoulder and dug his way up. I knew I would have some minor punctures from the sharp points of his nails, but I was willing to undergo some pain to keep from destroying his confidence. I still had visions of him sitting on my shoulder, in rhinestone collar and leash.

He put his head under my hair and the touch of his cool skin made the chills slide down my spine. He was facing behind me and I walked toward the mirror to see exactly what was going on. I lifted a handful of hair and looked. He was curled around my neck like a lover's arm. He stayed still.

I took a walk around the room slow, and he rode, digging into my back and neck with his nails. I wished he had passion instead of fear. I stayed clear of furniture and did a few slow twirls

– our first dance. I held the hem of my shorts like I was lifting a skirt – Cinderella with her prince.

His bright green tail was close to my cheek and I thought of the power he had in it, but he sat quiet, if not loving, until I bent and lowered my shoulder to the couch where he hopped off and sat staring up at me. I couldn't tell what kind of a look it was, but I felt a little understanding between us.

I dabbed Neosporin on my scratches and went to get the dirty clothes together to wash them while I showered and ate and got ready to go to the gym for my workout.

When I walked into the laundry room I saw my friend, the guy who'd helped me catch Ignats when he escaped. I'd waved to him a few times, but never stopped to have a conversation after that day. He was busy stuffing sheets and towels into a washer. I lugged my basket over to a nearby machine. He turned when he heard my steps.

"Hi there," I said. "Nice evening for laundry."

He looked distracted. I saw recognition flash on his face. "Oh. Iguana Woman," he said. He let out a short hyena laugh. "How is the rascal?"

"I had him perched on my shoulders a little while ago," I said. "We waltzed."

"Looks like he got a little frisky." He pointed to the red scratches on my clavicle.

"He wanted to lead." I laughed. "He was fine once he got situated. Pretty soon I'll have him doing the lambada."

"Can I watch?" He did the wild laugh again. "By the way, I'm Ivan."

I said I was Ramona and the rascal was Ignats. "You can call me Iguana Woman if you want. I kind of like that."

"Certainly." He looked at me like he thought I was weird, but enjoyed it. He invited me for some coffee and cake while we waited. He said he'd bought a chocolate cannoli cake from the Italian bakery and didn't want to eat it all himself. It was too rich to pass up. I could always save my frozen pot pie.

I followed him into his living room with my empty basket and laundry detergent and set them down beside the door. Instantly I

saw that I'd been lured there for a reason. He'd taken a good
guess that I was a sucker. A few feet away was a box filled with
breathing furry mounds in black and white and tan.

"Oh, yes," Ivan said. "I found these kittens behind my
apartment."

"No mother?"

"No sign of one. I've been looking for a few days. They eat
and drink on their own."

I bent down and picked up one wriggler. It was warm. It
looked up with round green eyes. I counted five others in the box.
Ivan bent down and scooped up two. He was holding them against
his blue silk shirt and one licked at the fabric and made a wet
spot.

"I guess you're looking for homes," I said.

"The truth is I was going to ask you to take all of them – but
just for a week or so. I have to go out of town tomorrow and I've
already tried all my friends. When I saw you in the laundry I felt
I'd been given a last chance."

"No problem. I owe you," I said. It was fine, a good excuse
to take home the darling babies, pets that would have to submit to
my kissing and cuddling. "I'll keep them until we find permanent
homes, if you want. Some of the nurses might take them."

"That would be lovely. I do a lot of traveling. And I'm not
really an animal person.'

I didn't understand un-animal people, but I had a good feeling
for Ivan. We sat at the ends of his dining room table and he lit
two tall beeswax candles between us. His apartment was starkly
furnished with square white couches and light wood chairs. An
evenly spaced row of brightly painted portraits continued from
wall to wall, surrounding the room and striping it in color. There
was a bronze antique lamp with three camels, sort of Siamese
triplets joined at the rump, sharing fancy draping that represented
a seat, with a lamp post growing out of the center. I told Ivan
how interesting it was and beautiful. I pointed out the draping as
particularly delicate.

"Yes. I love it too," he said, "their cascading carapacian livery."

"Uh huh." I laughed. "That's what I was about to say."

He had two stained glass Tiffany lamps and several blown glass vases from Florence.

Florence started me thinking of Enzo. He'd mentioned that some of his family still lived in Italy. It was one of the few things I knew about him. I doubted if they had taste like this. Enzo's apartment had matching furniture I recognized from newspaper ads. I was sure his only interest in decor was to make sure he had something to fuck on and eat on, preferably at the same time.

Ivan brought out two modest-sized pieces of cake. It was yellow sponge with chocolate cream on the inside and whipped cream with slivered almonds on the outside. The yellow part was moist and sweet with the flavor of rum.

Ivan's taste was clearly refined beyond suites of matching sofas and end tables. There was something pure and romantic about his place, like he set the scene for a movie. I was six feet across the table from him, looking at his face framed in the glow of two tall burning candles, eating spongecake with a chilled silver fork off delicate white china.

"I think it's synchronicity the way we ran into each other tonight, don't you?"

"What do you mean?"

"The first time we met, I helped capture your wild creature, and now you've appeared just in time to care for my helpless kittens."

"I guess so – two rescues."

"Now if we could save ourselves, everything would be perfect." He laughed in his abandoned style. I joined in, but couldn't match his volume.

I took another bite and thought of Enzo again, the contrast with Ivan. Enzo would have served our plates on the couch or in bed and he'd be picking crumbs off my body and eating them. I felt a hot wave at the thought. Enzo tasted every crumb he found, whether he could identify it or not. He was brazen even with things that didn't count.

Ivan said something that I missed – I was so filled up with Enzo, there was barely room to fit a friend.

Ivan and I folded our laundry together and then I took the

kittens to my apartment and put the box on its side in the bathroom with food and water handy. I closed the door to keep the other animals away.

Ivan asked if I needed a cage for Ignats. He had a carpenter friend who would do a good job for a reasonable price. I figured it was a good idea to keep Ignats in the window where he could get sun. He needed a glassed-in section to hold warmth when the temperature dropped. Ivan said he'd take care of it for me. It was hard to think of him with a carpenter friend, but then, Ivan was becoming my friend, and that seemed unusual.

He gave me a hug when he left and put his cheek against mine. "Take care," he said. "I'll make you lunch sometime and we can chat."

I was just in time to head to the gym. I started on my workout and was sweating my last couple of squats with sixty pounds, thinking I was never going to get anywhere, when I saw Dennis walk up behind me in the mirror. His tanned quads shone glossy. I wanted to put my hand on one of those hard mothers and give it a squeeze.

I nodded to him and put the bar up on the pegs. "What's up?" I said. I thought of the last posture he'd seen me in and took my time to even up the bar across the pegs, not wanting to watch the memory come into his eyes.

"Not much," he said. "We've been wondering if we'd see you back on the boat one of these days."

"Sure. Soon as I get the time and money." I wondered who the "we" was. Dennis and Charlie? Steve? Maybe just the kind of *we* to keep the conversation impersonal. I did crave to get back into that ocean. I got a rush of tingles in my stomach that fast, just thinking about it.

Dennis sat down at the next bench over and picked up the bar. It had a twenty on each side, so that meant he was doing eighty-five for starters.

I looked at Dennis's arms. They were much bigger than Enzo's. "You living with Enzo now?"

I picked the bar off the rack for an extra set and shook my head no to let the subject drop. I felt sheepish. I didn't want

Dennis, or anybody, to know anything about me and Enzo. "I think I'll try to get in a dive next weekend," I told Dennis. "Maybe we can buddy up."

"Yeah, maybe," he said. It didn't sound hopeful. I got a pang in the chest. He was what you'd call wholesome, somebody who would have been good for me. I pictured Enzo in his shining black speedos. He sure filled them out.

Dennis started on his routine, so I went to the far corner to do my dead lifts and stop thinking about him and the fun we'd had. Rory came over to see how I was doing. He helped me get my form just right, keep the buttocks tucked.

"You're doing fine," he said. "Takes time."

"It's hopeless," I told him. "Really hopeless."

"Not," he said. He whispered, "I can get you the juice. Anytime. Just a little down payment – whatever you need."

I felt a rush – time to take the step. "Get it," I said. "I'm ready."

That night at work I was busy assisting with lacerations and concussions and one critical case of abuse, a woman in her twenties whose boyfriend had beaten her with a tire tool. The policewoman came to get the details, but the woman stopped talking. She was afraid they'd take the guy away, lock him up so he couldn't get to her – and she couldn't get back to him.

I knew what she was feeling, wanting to be free and not wanting to. I started thinking of all I'd bitten off for myself, the charges for the gym and the diving classes. Now I was going into debt with Enzo for my first month of steroids. I'd caught myself in a net – or stepped under it willingly, like the female lobster following the male.

My head filled with thoughts of the clear blue depths I was missing, ghostly fingered staghorn corals and waving purple sea fans, schooling black and yellow striped sergeant majors and cruising multi-colored parrotfish, their scales outlined in pastels, as if painted. That depth of blue was behind it all, waiting for me, the space where anything could lurk.

I drove over to Enzo's the next evening. I'd already had my

workout, but I couldn't unwind. I kept flexing, hardening my whole body. I didn't want to owe him.

I unlocked the door of his house and walked in. I could smell that great aroma from the kitchen. I went through the dining room on tiptoe. Enzo was simmering fresh garlic, olive oil, and wine, stirring with a wooden spoon. Steam was pouring upward into the stove fan from a boiling pot of spaghetti. I could see the oven was on and knew it had fresh, crusty garlic bread in it. Two servings of salad and a bottle of red wine were sitting on the counter top.

I tiptoed behind him and put my arm around his shoulder, stretched to give him a kiss. He jerked and his hand came up holding the spoon like a club.

"Christ!" he yelled. He threw the spoon into the sink where it splashed into a bowl of sudsy water.

He looked angry from overreacting, but it was kind of cute, his being startled.

"I'm sorry," I said. "I just wanted a kiss."

"Fuck, Ramona," he said.

"Okay," I told him.

"You scared the piss out of me."

"I'm sorry," I said, "I didn't know you were so high-strung."

"Jesus, you're lucky I didn't splash hot oil on you."

"I'm always lucky."

"Lucky you ran into me." He grabbed my hair and stuck his face under it and growled into my neck. I felt his hot breath and smooth lips and the chills started to run. He stopped and watched while I caught my breath.

"Food's ready," he said. He turned back to the stove and wiped sweat off his upper lip. I wondered what he wasn't telling me, why he was jumpy.

We took the stuff in to the living room and set it on the coffee table in front of the TV. Enzo moved next to me and put his tongue in my ear and bit the lobe between his top teeth and bottom lip. He'd told me that way it didn't hurt. It did, but just enough, just right. He slid his mouth around to mine and stuck his tongue in. I melted into the heat of his mouth.

"Let's take our clothes off," he whispered. "Can't get sauce on your uniform."

I pulled my whites over my head without a blink and whipped off my bra and white pantyhose. I picked up my salad and sat on the couch to wait for his next course.

He had his shorts down to his ankles, and wasn't wearing any kind of briefs. He flung off the shorts with one kick and sat close. He reached behind me.

I sucked in air with the sensation when he found my ass and stuck his finger in. He worked it in and out lightly while I held onto my salad, not wanting to move to put it down. After a few minutes he removed the finger, took my salad away and turned me around.

I got on my hands and knees on the couch waiting for his hard cock. He was busy doing something back there. He put a hand on my hip and hunched over me. His cock came up against my ass and I waited for him to slip it down into my wet cunt. Instead I felt his fingers holding my cheeks apart and the sharp burning as he pushed into my sphincter.

"Easy, easy," he said.

I smelled olive oil and I knew he had greased himself up, but as slow as he worked it, I felt like I was ripping apart at the seam. I couldn't quiet a shriek of pain. "No, stop! I can't do it," I told him.

"Easy, relax. You'll enjoy it – if you relax." He gave me a little slap on the ass.

"I can't. It hurts. Stop." I tried to reach back to move him, but all I could do was grasp at his solid thighs. I couldn't move myself an inch and he pounded faster. I sobbed with the searing. I was sure I was bleeding. He kept going. Finally he stopped and let out a guttural sigh. He shuddered and slowly withdrew, and I collapsed onto my stomach. Enzo rolled to my side and kissed my shoulder. He put his arm around me.

I closed my eyes.

When I sat up he was lighting a cigarette. I'd never seen him smoke. I detested smoke.

"Guess I knocked you out, huh?"

I rubbed my eyes and pulled a strand of hair away from my lips. "You hurt me, Enzo."

He motioned me to turn over. "Let me look."

I rolled onto my side away from him and felt his hand spreading my cheeks apart gently.

"You're fine – you're just not used to it. I was real careful."

"I don't want to get used to it."

"You will – once you learn to relax. You'll beg me for it."

I gave him a look and got up and went into the bathroom and checked myself. I didn't trust his judgment. True, I wasn't bleeding, but it still stung.

I came back with a decision to make him promise that he would never do that again or it would be the end of us. He was chewing a mouthful of pasta and reached out to tousle my hair as I sat down. I saw he was wet from washing himself in the kitchen. I picked up my plate and thought about what to say. I wasn't sure he'd even care if I stopped coming by. I thought about putting on my clothes and leaving without a word. I couldn't do it.

He swallowed and started twisting another huge bite on his fork. "I was wondering if you wanted to make some extra money. I heard about a possibility."

"Diving?"

He nodded.

I slurped some angel hair. My spirits picked up. "I'm in bad shape financially." I told him I owed more than I could handle on my credit cards already, for the diving lessons and the gym membership. "There's nothing I'd rather do than make diving my profession."

"Ordinarily, there's not much money in it. You have to work all the angles." He stretched his neck. "I just happen to be the hottest guy in the world when it comes to business."

Drugs popped into my head immediately. Since I'd moved to Florida, that's all I'd heard about. But I didn't think Enzo would involve me in anything. If that's what it was, I'd just tell him to forget it.

"If I could get some work diving, I wouldn't have to pay to get in the water, and I'd have the extra money. It would be ideal."

"Uh huh. I thought of asking you the day of the rescues. You never panicked in all that mess."

I shrugged. "No time to."

"I still want to give you the money for your bodybuilding. It would help for the diving. I'd love to see you with muscles," he said. He poked my left biceps. "You'd be bigger than life, right out of the movies. Still couldn't handle me though. Nobody can."

His face was level with mine. He was smiling. "How bout an advance? What do you need? How much?"

"I don't know. I haven't figured it out."

He was looking at me with his lips clamped, like he had an idea. He went into the bedroom and came back. He held out a thick handful of twenties. "Take it. It'll get you started," he said.

I felt my eyes bugging – I wasn't used to people having that much cash around the house. I wondered if he considered it to be paying me for the sex. Heat went to my face. "I don't know. I'd rather wait and get the job. I wouldn't have to borrow."

"It'll be a while. I want you to start building up – so you're ready to do the work." He put his arm around me and pulled my face against his chest. "You're beautiful – and special. I want to see exactly what you're capable of."

I put down my plate and hugged him tight. I could feel the warmth flowing inside me. I'd do whatever he said to stay like that, to have times like that forever. I wanted to show him what I had inside me. I knew I was special, but I'd never had the chance to show it. Nobody ever believed in me before.

He kissed me and then moved me aside by the shoulders to take another bite of his pasta.

"What kind of diving would it be?"

"Easy stuff. I'll let you know when I get the details."

I nuzzled into his neck and kissed his ear. I pushed the money back into his hand. "Thanks, I appreciate it. But I won't borrow money from you unless I can be sure of the job. I wouldn't want to stick you."

"Why not? I'll stick you every chance I get." He took my plate of pasta and set it on the table. I could see the sexual glaze in his eyes.

I felt tears come into mine. I was afraid he'd hurt me again, but I couldn't say anything.

He pulled my hair back so my chin was pointed up at him. He smiled. "Sweetheart, I'm not gonna hurt you. We don't have to use the backdoor every time." His hand went down and lightly stroked my pussy.

"I want you to have the money," he said. "Let's fuck on it – it's better than a handshake."

He got hard fast and I thought, Jesus, what have I gotten into.

"I'm getting hot just thinking of you with all those muscles," he said. He started working his way down with his mouth and I kept mine shut.

21

◆◆◆◆◆◆◆◆◆◆◆◆◆◆◆◆

I was in the gym pumping that bar by noon the next day. I told Rory I was ready for the juice. I knew I'd made a deal with the devil and I just wanted to get on with it before the stakes became too clear.

During my second set of bench presses a hand with a syringe appeared above my head. I put the bar in the rack and glanced around. I craned my neck backwards.

"Jesus, Rory, aren't you afraid somebody will walk in?"

"I locked the door."

"Oh," I said. I had a weird feeling.

"You ready for it?" Rory asked.

"Yeah. I think so. I get one cc of the Primobolin and one Dianabol tab, right?"

"And the ten cc's." He laughed.

"Ten?" I asked.

In a second, his tone cued me in, that he was referring to a ten cc ejaculation, the average amount. It was something I learned in nursing school and we used to joke about. I couldn't figure why Rory would know that. Maybe he was in the habit of measuring everything.

"Here's your D-bol." He handed me a white tablet and I took it in my palm and walked over to the water fountain. My stomach was churning on the way back. I wondered why it hadn't crossed my mind there was going to be some kind of string. He'd said he wasn't making money off me.

"You want it," he whispered as I stood in front of him. "I've seen you looking at me."

I stared. Rory was a Greek sculpture in his tights. The smooth tan skin showing on his chest, arms, and thighs glistened in the fluorescent lighting. I didn't want him though, not even a flicker.

"I have to look," I said. "You've created yourself for looking."

He had set a brown glass bottle, a plastic bottle of rubbing alcohol, and cotton balls on the bench next to me while he opened another syringe and stuck the needle upside down into the rubber seal on the vial. He knew what he was doing. He pushed air into the bottle and then drew the liquid into the syringe. The needle was medium, probably a twenty-two gauge.

There it was, inches away, the remedy for my weakness. I swallowed my anxiety.

"Juice is nice." Rory drew the needle out slowly and held it in front of me to squeeze a drop onto the tip. "Peel me a glut," he said.

I didn't hesitate to think. I pulled my tights down halfway on the right buttocks. He tilted alcohol onto a cotton ball with one hand and wiped the injection site. I watched his forearms, smooth and hairless and strong with a light sheen of moisture. He put the needle to my skin and pushed the plunger to penetrate at an angle. I took the prick without a blink. It was cold and then started to burn as he pushed all the liquid into the muscle. I felt a miniature lightning bolt transferring its energy. He had good technique with the needle. He finished and withdrew, then swabbed the spot again with alcohol. I pulled my tights back into place.

He set the vial and used syringe on the floor and pushed me down onto the bench. It wasn't rough, but my strength was non-existent against him. "Rory, stop," I said. "This wasn't in the deal."

A glaze came over his eyes, like giving that shot had really turned up his heat and he was just barely controlling. He had the refined muscle memory from all his years of training to know just how much force was needed. He knew my small strength.

The light scent of his body drifted down and I could feel the radiation of his warmth. My hips rocked involuntarily toward him on the plastic cushion of the bench and I caught myself and tensed, but I felt myself tingling with lubrication. The ripples were tight in the smooth clear skin of his abdomen as he eased down. He was beautiful and I wasn't afraid of him. He'd seen the movement of my hips and locked onto that cue.

"No, Rory." It came out weak. "No, I mean it." I was breathless and he knew it.

"Look, baby." He pulled on his shorts with one hand and his cock sprang out shining. "Eight inches long, six and a half around."

He wasn't exaggerating.

"Don't you wanna make it part of the deal?"

I didn't want him, but I started to imagine the feeling, the hardness shoved into the wet gnawing space. He put a hand into the crotch of my short tights and his fingers slipped inside. His eyes registered my wetness. His mouth opened.

I decided to give him a reason he could understand, even if it might not be true. "I have a boyfriend," I said. "You know Enzo. He used to come here."

A change came over his face. Lines ran across his smooth forehead.

"You and Enzo?"

"Your friend. We're going together."

"Friend? Huh uh. Enzo's nobody's friend."

I didn't know what to say to that. I felt a twinge of fear. He was rethinking while his fingers moved inside me. A hard shine slid over his eyes. "Give my regards to Enzo."

I was rigid and the tension just sped up the heat that was collecting between us.

"Come now, baby. Come on." He lowered himself closer and his fingers peeled my tights down below my knees and off, while I lay there staring. I put a hand up to his chest to keep him back, one meager try, and the warm wall of his power cut off my thinking. I didn't even have the mental strength to try to stop him.

He plunged into me and filled me up tight. He moved

mechanically in a smooth rhythm that filled up my brain. I was swirling inside myself with anger and guilt and a pure physical pleasure I couldn't deny, didn't want. Didn't want to stop.

He lifted his heavy thigh from across the bench and pulled himself out of me slowly. I propped myself on my elbows and shuddered as my body came back to normal.

Rory adjusted himself back into his shorts and picked up the vial, syringe, discarded wrapper, and cotton ball. "I'll put your juice where it'll be safe," he said. He walked toward the door and unlocked it, then went behind the desk and into his office.

I realized that's how he intended to handle it, with silence. When it was over it was if nothing had happened. All right. It hadn't. I pulled my tights back up and put my hands to the bar for my last set. One fuck, two fuck, three fuck, four . . . all the way to twelve without a pause.

When I left Rory was doing his squats with another guy spotting for him. He didn't notice me, and I didn't say a word.

I got to Enzo's that night in time for pasta and bed before work. I could smell the garlic, but the kitchen light was off so I followed the glow into the bedroom. Enzo was stretched out on his back with a paperback across his naked groin. He was in a comfortable snooze. A glass of red wine was on the nightstand. I stripped and snuggled in next to him and he put an arm and a leg over me. For a few seconds I felt loved and protected.

He opened his eyes and stroked my hair back from my face, swirling it behind my ear. "What's up, Ramona?"

I breathed out some air. I wanted to tell him. "Tired," I said. "I worked out hard today. Got my first shot."

"Oh?" he said. "You need to eat. I made some chicken cacciatore with no fat or skin." He kissed my ear. I felt him getting hard and poking between my legs from behind. I tensed up, and he scooted down and slipped smoothly into place, making fireworks in my head, taking away most of my brain – except the guilty part.

I woke up in the same position with Enzo stroking my face again. He nibbled my neck. "Food," he said.

He gave me a soft slap on the rump and I rolled over and got up to drag myself after him.

He served me a big portion of chicken while I sipped my wine.

"Got you a job," Enzo said. He cut off a piece of breast meat and put it in his mouth.

"Oh yeah?" I answered through a mouthful. I slurped in a strand of pasta and wiped my chin with my finger. "Diving?"

"Uh huh."

I swallowed and waited while Enzo chewed. I was already scared, but thinking a lot about money, getting steroids elsewhere, and membership at a different gym.

"It helps that you're building up. I told the boss you were a bodybuilder. He wasn't too thrilled about having a woman, but I convinced him you were tough." He reached over and squeezed my right biceps.

I smiled and flexed it and made it roll. I'd always been able to do that, but it looked firmer to me already. "What do I have to do?"

"Nothing strenuous, if everything works. A little search and recovery. We go together. You won't have any problem."

"Search and recovery?" Something moved in my stomach. It wasn't the chicken.

"Yeah. Nothing to it." He picked up a chicken leg and slurped off a piece of meat. "You learned the techniques in class."

"Yeah. I remember." I watched the red sauce on his chin.

He looked into my eyes and wiped his mouth. "It's good pay."

I nodded. I didn't want to know how much money he was talking. I didn't want him to sense my fears.

"It's in the Bahamas. Excellent visibility. We can take a long weekend. Just play most of the time. Ever been to Bimini?"

"No. Never made it." I pictured white sand and clear blue water, a Nassau grouper feeding from my hand, or even a shining spotted moray. Pure clear water and friendly fish. The work was just something to get through. When it was over, it would be like it never existed.

"It'll be an adventure. Trust me, Ramona. I've done it half a dozen times, no problem."

I almost trusted him. My only problem was a square black package I visualized tilted against a rock. I didn't have the imagination to figure out what kind of drugs might be inside. I pushed aside the thought of myself as a link in the drug chain that led to ruined lives.

Enzo was smiling and chatty. "We leave Friday morning. There'll be some tourists and crew – a commercial dive boat – but the two of us will go alone by dingy on the night dive. Captain Blondie will fill in the details when we get there."

"Captain Blondie?" I knew it was the sleazeball from the dive boat. Everything was clear.

I woke up at noon on the day I was due for my second dose of juice. I felt the dread of seeing Rory and had a sick feeling about the job with Enzo. Fuck. I got myself out of bed on fantasies. Maybe Rory would be too busy to fuck me, and Enzo's job was anchor recovery.

I went to the gym as scheduled. I kept up a hot pace, barely resting in between sets. I wondered if the steroids were giving me the extra push or if it was the fire in my stomach.

I'd almost finished my workout when Rory's tight torso pressed into my shoulders. His cock moved hard against the small of my back. I watched in the mirror as his mouth came down on my neck and started the chills, and his hand rose up with the prepared syringe. He slid down my tights with the other hand, and I felt the cool swipe of alcohol across my ass, as he continued sucking my skin between his lips. He was a strange combo of caretaker and vampire. We locked eyes in the mirror as he pushed the plunger and I held steady for the sting. The cold-hot trickle of the Primo penetrated my hip.

He pulled back and motioned for me to take off my clothes. A wave of heat ran through me with his gesture. I whipped down my tights and lay flat on the nearest bench. The faster, the less passion. I'd have the money in another week and then I could pay him for the rest of the cycle and start giving my own shots, never come back to his gym.

I asked off work Thursday through Monday, telling the nurse manager I was going diving in the Bahamas. Suddenly it felt real, vacation days. She was happy I was recovering from my marriage break up. The truth was I rarely thought about Gary anymore, except when he called. I was in a different universe.

I went in early to do my workout on Thursday. I was due for a rest day, but since I would have to miss the weekend, I wanted to get it all in, upper, lower and cardio, not to lose ground. I was starting to see a difference. My legs were more cut above the knees.

When Rory finished the ritual and dropped the syringe, I was on him. I let the energy of my anger take over as I stripped him down and pushed him back on the bench and worked him hard squeezing my vagina. I felt the strength in my quads as I slid easily on his erection. If I had to do it, I was going to do it myself.

His face contorted like he was flexing, and I came hot and wet in an angry seething. I felt relief. I resolved to do my job over the weekend with that same vigor, and do it well. Then I'd never do it again.

Later that evening I saw Ivan and he said he'd feed the kittens and iguana while I was gone. I asked him inside to go over the feeding procedures.

"You're my savior again," I said.

He reminded me that they were his kittens originally, so we were still even.

I told him Ignats probably wouldn't eat much and it didn't matter if he ate at all. Iguanas only needed to eat twice a week. I showed him how to grate the squash and mix the monkey biscuit and set the small dish in the corner under the sofa. Ig was already fed for the day, but I held the dish under his chin.

"He won't eat this," I said to Ivan.

Ignats slid his tongue toward the squash and tasted a sliver. Immediately he bobbed his head to the food and began to scoop it between his jaws like I hadn't fed him in a month. Ivan laughed so loud that Ignats froze to watch.

"You can't force it," Ivan said. "Just free yourself up to accept the good things when they happen."

"I tend to push," I said.

Ivan smiled and nodded like he knew I couldn't take his advice.

He let it rest. "I think Jack has your cage almost ready," he said.
I can have him bring it over while you're gone. If we can, we'll
put Ignats inside."

"That would be great. I'll give you the money for the cage
when I get home."

"No rush," he said. "I trust you."

22

◆◆◆◆◆◆◆◆◆◆◆◆◆◆◆◆◆

We left the Port of Miami on Friday morning. There were six divers on board the sixty-foot dive boat, and Captain Blondie and the cook, besides Enzo and me. Blondie's long, streaky blond hair looked even dirtier than when I'd seen him on the *Sharkbiter*. I noticed he wore a diamond stud earring. The cook looked like his older brother.

Enzo and I had loaded up the rental equipment, hauled on the ice, and helped the small group of tourists aboard, normal divemaster chores. I lugged those 80's like they were styrofoam rather than heavy gauge aluminum. I kept convincing myself I'd imagined the drug thing and we'd be doing honest work to make our money.

I started to enjoy the coolness of the salt spray on my face and remember that I was on my way to the Bahamas, doing my first job as a divemaster, a fantasy come true.

The captain said we were making fifteen knots and would be in Bimini in about three and a half hours. The plan was to tie up at Weech's dock, clear customs, have a sandwich, and make an afternoon dive near Turtle Rocks. Those were three islands just south of Bimini with a nice ledge and plenty of fish. Likely spot for lobster. We'd dock again for the evening and have a cookout.

Enzo said after everything was cleaned up and ready for the morning dive, we could go drinking and dancing if we wanted.

The Compleat Angler was there, the historic bar where Ernest
Hemingway used to hang out. They always had a calypso band
on Friday nights.

There was nothing at all suspicious in our schedule. It was at
least another day before I had to start worrying.

Enzo reminded me that we were crossing the Gulf Stream –
venturing into the Devil's Triangle. I thought, shit, I'd been living
in a devil's triangle for days with him and Rory. Fathoms of water
didn't scare me.

I was energized by the wind we were creating and the loud
thrum of the diesel engines. The sky was blue and the slant of the
sun turned the ocean into swells and peaks of wrinkled mercury. By
the time we lost sight of the buildings nothing mattered but our
very small boat powering its course across the heavy silver flow.

It seemed a short time till the captain sighted land. It was just
a brown haze in the distance that gradually grew to be beach and
trees with a crest topped by two buildings. Enzo said those were
condos that would never be finished. We headed toward the island
and soon the captain lined up the range markers, two telephone
poles with orange tops. We followed the line until we passed the
sandbar and turned to take a parallel course to the beach. Enzo
put up the Q-flag and courtesy flag.

We turned into the harbor and passed some pretty pastel
buildings and other dilapidated ones. I saw the sign for Weech's,
and two guys, one black and one white, came out to help us dock.
The twin engines whirred against the tide and we glided into the
slip, threw our lines, and stopped in a broil of reverse.

Enzo and I were instructed to set up tanks. We handed our
passports over to the captain to take to customs. I felt the hairs
move on the back of my neck without a breeze.

That afternoon we helped the last pair of divers into the water,
a woman and her three-hundred-fifty pound husband. I figured
diving must be one of the few sports where fitness could be ignored
– until there was a problem. Enzo and I had a break until the first
pair came back up again. I was antsy to get in the water, but Enzo
said it wasn't part of the job. I sat on the gunwhale and watched
the sparkling blue, followed the divers' bubbles near the bow.

The captain was forward. Enzo walked over and reached a finger up the back of my bikini. He pulled me toward him for a kiss. I let myself relax into him.

"Good job so far, baby," he told me. "Keep it up and I'll see you get a call for every trip."

"Good training. Nothing to it."

I saw his face change. "The real job's tomorrow – you got that big guy in the water, you can handle it."

"All I did was hold his hand when he stepped onto the transom." I could feel my lightheartedness slipping away with the words.

"Don't worry," Enzo said. "I'll be right there with you. No problem."

I looked at the water and I could still see the air rolling to the surface. The group must have been watching something nearly under the boat, or else the current was moving the bubbles our way. The water was clear and calm. I wanted to go down and stay there.

Nobody came up with any lobster. I wondered if Blondie had even tried to put them in a likely place. Entertaining tourists didn't seem to be his major interest. We motored back to Weech's and he sent me and Enzo off to buy fish to put on the grill along with the hot dogs.

As we stepped out to the road Enzo took my hand. It surprised me. We were the picture of regular lovers on vacation, happy in love. For a second I let myself imagine, but I knew Enzo had no similar fantasies.

I'd never seen a place like Bimini. Never been to an island. Enzo said we were in Alicetown, the only town. We strolled down the street with the other tourists, the white people. We were dressed like them, me in shorts and bathing suit top, Enzo with his fish T-shirt, but I knew we were out of place.

We passed stalls along the side of the road with women selling bread, straw crafts, and T-shirts shredded into patterns of strands to let the air in. They rippled in the breeze. Enzo picked out a red one and bought it for me. He said he wanted to see how sexy I'd look in it. I wondered if he could sense my negative feelings.

We came to a small wooden building with a bookdrop carved
out of its heavy, peeling door. Enzo opened the door and we
stepped in. Light came from a window and there was a musty,
damp, book smell. The room was lined with filled shelves, and a
table in the middle had a ledger with titles and the names of
borrowers, on the honor system. It felt safe and friendly. I picked
up a book on Jacques Cousteau.

"Let's go," Enzo said. "We need to find the conch lady before
it gets too late."

I remembered that everything was a job, with the hardest one
to come. We left the library and walked farther on the narrow
gravel road, past the small arch and path that led to the door of
The Compleat Angler, past the large modern arch to the Big Game
Club. We had to step into the sand to give the cars room to pass.
I kept forgetting the traffic drove on the left – Enzo had to save my
life twice. I wondered how many more times he could manage it.

He went inside a small grocery and I waited while Enzo asked
the woman if she knew where to find the conch lady. Her musical
voice was teasing and soothing and I just listened and let my eyes
wander the counter over the browned clumps of coconut candy
and tiny bottles with hot peppers in oil. I passed up firm, dense
slices of banana bread, but couldn't resist the smooth solid loaves
of warm white bread. I wished I could buy one of everything,
including a bottle of rum, and sit under a palm tree on the beach
forever. Let that evil package rot wherever it was.

We found the conch lady at home, a thin, pretty woman in a
flowered dress. She brought out four small dolphin and a plastic
bag of conch. We bought it all and headed back to the boat. I
kept thinking of how it could be, if Enzo and I were here alone
without the tentacles of Miami. We could lose ourselves in food
and drink, music and sea, take it all in and make love out of it.
Sure.

I looked at Enzo. I could see in his face what he was thinking.
He was just going through the paces, waiting for the time I
dreaded. It was a thrill for him. I could sense it. He was part of
the cold undercurrent of the tropics. He was for Enzo, nobody
else. He was only with me because I was with him, handy. My

stomach felt oily and I thought about two tourists who'd thrown up crossing the Gulf Stream. If only my nausea were that simple.

We marinated the conch in lemon and grilled it and the fish on the patio at the dock. The conch was chewy, but everyone said delicious. We had corn and salad. I couldn't taste any of it. I drank several beers. To me it felt like my last supper as a fucking free citizen.

We danced and drank yellow birds at the Angler that night. I partied it up, a last fling. I was weaving on the way back to the boat, feeling good, when terror sprang into me. I grabbed Enzo and turned him to face me. I gave him a hard kiss then held on around his neck. He held me for a minute and then pulled back. He looked at me and smoothed my hair roughly. He knew I was freaking.

"Don't tell me you're gonna chicken out now," he said. I could see a glare in his eyes even by moonlight.

"I don't know what the real job is. I'm scared to death that it's something illegal." I had hopes that he would tell me there was nothing wrong, that I had misinterpreted the whole thing.

"Don't worry. I'll give you the details tomorrow. It's easy – just our own private night dive. We can do it naked, if you want."

I put my hands over my face and closed my eyes. "What about the other divers?"

"Most of 'em will be at the bars by then. None of their business where we go."

I shook my head.

"Buck up, Ramona. I don't think Blondie's giving any free tickets back to Miami."

I caught the tone of it and at that moment I realized that I'd already gone too far. I felt a shiver run through me. Enzo wasn't on my side. He had no loyalty to me, regardless of our sexual intimacy. If I caused a problem, it wouldn't bother him to let Blondie fix it.

He squeezed me and grabbed my ass. "Let's do dive naked." He opened his mouth and wiggled his tongue from side to side. "What d'ya think?"

"I think I'm insane."

23

◆◆◆◆◆◆◆◆◆◆◆◆◆◆◆◆◆

At any other time in my life sleeping on a boat in the Bahamas would have been a dream, but the soft rolling couldn't soothe me that night. I woke up in my cramped bunk with hot pieces of horror racing through my brain, whirling patterns that made me feel like air wasn't getting into my lungs. I didn't dare close my eyes again, and I lay there frozen, gasping sometimes, watching Enzo breathe softly in the opposite bunk, until dawn. I must have drifted off because I woke up smelling bacon and coffee. My stomach turned.

All day I had a hard time keeping track of what I was doing, and Enzo could see it. He told me to relax and do my job with the tourists. I could make a dive with them if I wanted. I didn't want to. Everything about me was off kilter. I just wanted to get back home.

After dinner everybody else drifted into town. The captain told me and Enzo to follow him to his cabin. We sat side by side on the bunk while he dug into a canvas bag and brought out a small zippered pouch that he handed to Enzo.

"Same routine as always," he said. "This time the numbers are twenty-five, thirty-six, twenty-two, and seventy-nine, eighteen, fifty-seven. Got it?"

Enzo repeated the numbers while I looked at him, wondering what kind of crazy measurements they were. I thought of telling the captain I didn't understand a thing and maybe they should cut me out.

"Red float this time," Blondie said.

"Got it. Piece of cake," Enzo said. He squeezed my shoulder, but hardened his eyes to give me a message. "With Ramona along nobody will give us a thought. She's so wholesome." He pinched my cheek and I tried to smile. "Hell of a good dive buddy too."

Captain Blondie lowered his eyes to my tits then down to the crotch of my bathing suit, and he licked his upper lip. Enzo ignored it.

"Uh huh," Blondie said. "Whatever you say, Enzo. Just get the job done."

I thought of flipping him a bird, but he reached back into his bag and brought out a hard leather case. I knew what it was from the shape. I could feel myself shaking when Enzo took it and weighed it in his hand. I looked at his face. He was smiling down at the gun. "All set," he said. His eyes were bright.

"We don't need that." I put my hand on Enzo's forearm and pushed it back toward the captain.

Enzo released my fingers. "Captain's orders, Mona. Just a macho thing. Never gonna use it."

I was shaking, but I straightened up. "Let's get going."

The divers were all still ashore, as Enzo had predicted. We pulled the dinghy to the stern and transferred our gear into it, along with a fuel can, extra line, lobstering gear, and spearguns for cover. It was a fifteen-foot hard boat so there was room to stow the precious packages of nightmares. Enzo gave the cord a pull. It was only a nine horsepower engine and we chugged slowly away not to draw attention. A half moon slipped in and out of the clouds and parts of the sky were specked with stars. The water was glass. Fucking perfect conditions for a night dive.

We hugged the north side of the inlet since we were running without lights. Then Enzo cut across and we headed past South Bimini toward Turtle Rocks again. It was a short way and I didn't say a word. I was shivering in the warm humid air.

When we passed the third small island, Enzo opened the square case and took out a piece of electronic equipment. "GPS.

It's gonna take us right to our catch. I put in the lat and long and it gives us a heading."

He punched in the numbers the captain had given him. "Degrees . . . minutes . . . seconds . . . Okay." He hit the second set. "Now all we have to do is follow the course."

The heading and a map showing our position appeared on the screen and Enzo handed me a flashlight to shine on the compass mounted under my seat. He turned the dinghy a little to follow the course. "We've only got about four miles to go. The GPS will tell us how to correct if we need to."

I wasn't excited with the electronics. I just let him do his thing while I concentrated on telling myself it was only one time and would soon be over. I looked at our pile of gear and wondered where the other piece went.

Four miles took a long time. I started to wonder if we'd missed the mark.

"What if somebody else saw the float?" I said. "It seems pretty risky."

"No. For one thing, it's like any other lobster ball. Unlikely that somebody would bother it. Besides, it was way below the surface. The line was held down by a solenoid and battery attached to a timer." He looked at his watch. "Until fifteen minutes ago."

Something about his eyes and his bone structure in the moonlight scared me.

"It's an easy rig, and these guys have a lot of practice," he said. "You can bet that float didn't pop till it was due."

I spotted the fucking thing before Enzo even told me to start looking. It was twenty yards ahead on our port side, like a round pill on a mirror. At least we didn't have to spend time searching. There were no other boats in sight. We chugged up to the float and Enzo dropped anchor. We were surrounded by flickering chartreuse lights under the surface, little sizzling rings.

"Phosphorescence," Enzo said. "The nights are magic here."

While Enzo put the GPS away, I cracked my cyalume light, fastened it onto my tank, and wrestled into my BC. Then I helped him shrug into his vest. I asked why we couldn't just pull up the trap by the float line, like the lobster fishermen do.

"It's on a thin line. Another precaution."

"Makes sense," I said. "Let's get it up."

"Atta girl. I knew you had the spirit."

My spirit was shit, but I strapped my knife to my calf, and put on my mask and stuck the regulator into my mouth. I went backwards over the side into the cool water and headed down by the line to wait for Enzo on the bottom. It was against buddy rules. So what. Rules were fucked.

I had my light pointed ahead and saw the lobster trap growing larger beneath me. The plastic cover inside was white, not black like I'd imagined. No lobsters in there, something a hell of a lot more expensive per pound. I landed, put a little air in my vest for neutral buoyancy and perched myself on the box, one hand on the line. I checked my depth gauge. It read about fifty feet. That meant we had over an hour, plenty of time. I was past being frightened. I was angry enough at Enzo and myself to wipe out everything else.

Enzo touched down beside me and started pulling out the lift bags. He seemed to be in a hurry all of a sudden and I thought maybe the pressure was getting to him. There were four lift bags, one to hook on each corner. He handed me two and I watched while he tied it down and filled it off his regulator.

I tried to do the same. It was a clumsy job, holding the light and your breath and fixing the bag at the same time. Enzo was working at top speed and had two attached before my first one was filled. When we got the three on, the trap lifted from the bottom and with the fourth it began to rise. We each took a side and finned up, guiding the box between us. It was an easy swim. I shined my light on the trap to see how it was doing, then on Enzo. He wasn't wearing any trunks. He had a hard on that could have conducted a symphony. He knew I was looking. I heard him laugh through his regulator.

It gave me the creeps, how invulnerable he seemed. I looked to both sides as if somebody were watching. I thought about the easy meal he'd make, his perfect plump bait. He went to work in the ghostly green glow of the cyalume over his shoulder, releasing air a little at a time with the dump valves on the lift bags so the trap would continue to rise slowly as it got shallow.

We broke the surface and Enzo left the box hovering just below it. I filled my vest and held onto a corner. Enzo was at my ear.

"Stay low. Keep quiet. There's a boat – I think it's Bahamians fishing – a few hundred yards north."

I jerked around to look behind me. I could make out a boat with two men against the lights of Bimini in the distance. I felt sparks of panic flash through my skull.

"Enzo. Christ. Are they headed this way?"

"No. They're just drifting. I don't think they can see us, but if we splash around pulling that cage out of the water, they're sure to."

"What if they do? Huh? What do we say?" I caught some water in my throat on the last word and started to cough. I put my hand against my mouth and choked and panicked and choked some more. When I finally stopped I saw Enzo staring behind me in the direction of the boat. He dropped his weight belt and unhooked his vest. The vest floated away past me as he finned hard and lurched over the side into the dinghy. I saw his white cheeks go over.

I waited with the trap, not knowing what I was supposed to do and not daring to call out. I heard the clunk of the anchor inside the hull. The engine rumbled.

Enzo never said a word. I pushed off the side and the engine sputtered uncomfortably close to my feet as he turned. Then he was gone.

There I was hanging onto a crate of something illegal in the middle of the Atlantic. The only sign of land was a glow in the distance. The water was warm and smooth as glass. I could float until daylight. But what then? All I could think was that Enzo had left me there to be arrested – or shot. He had a gun. All these drug people probably had guns. If it wasn't the police, it could be anybody wanting to make a quick million or so. I had no idea how much the stuff was worth, but much more than my life, no doubt. Enzo knew the stakes and he'd made his choice.

I started to feel scattered, look around the blackness for
sharks. Think about Charlie, Dennis, Gary. What would they hear
happened to me? I was paying the price for taking my chances.
What was I after? It was hard to remember. Freedom, adventure,
control over my life – I'd fallen short of getting those. Something
else had sneaked in and taken over my mind.

It was a crazy thing to be thinking, clinging to an island of
dope in the middle of the ocean at midnight, but finally the
meaning of love became clear to me – take or be taken, use or be
used. Any variation was only by degree. There was no possible
equality of feelings. The loved one had all the advantages. Enzo,
the bastard – he goddamn fucking well knew it. But so did I. I'd
been on the high side of it with Gary.

I heard a motor. It wasn't Enzo's nine-horse. It got louder. The
only thing to do was plunge. I pulled the plastic balls to dump air
from the lift bags on my side of the trap. It started to sink slowly
at an angle and I finned up on it and slipped my mask back on
and stuck my regulator in my mouth. I pressed the button to
empty my vest and hung on.

I started to drop too quickly as the buoyancy decreased ten
feet under. For an instant I was on the edge of panic, my ears
becoming painful before I had time to clear. I shot some air into
my vest and slowed just enough. I blew hard into my ears until
the squeak of air made the pain stop. I wasn't ready to let go of the
package and drift off in the dark. If Enzo came back for it, he'd
find me.

The package hit and I touched bottom in total blindness.
There I was – nightdiving blind like Steve, desperate. I could
almost laugh.

The bottom was smooth at least, sandy, nothing rocky or
sharp with holes for morays. I heard the vibration of an engine
either approaching or above me. It was impossible to tell. I just
had to wait.

I figured I had about forty-five minutes of air left unless I'd
been breathing heavy. We'd taken ten minutes to bring up the
dope. I was glad I'd only filled one bag. I didn't dare flick on my
light to check the pressure gauge. I thought about bottom time,

residual nitrogen. It would be close, but why worry? When I came up they'd shoot me. I wouldn't have time to get bent.

I remembered the cyalume tied to my valve. I didn't think they could see it from the surface, but I wasn't sure. I yanked off the glowing chartreuse stick and stuck it into the crotch of my bikini to smother the glow.

I could still hear the engine puttering. I was breathing fast and I concentrated on settling myself down to conserve air. I tipped my mask to let some cool water onto my eyes, and then cleared again. I sat on the trap. I thought about the photograph of the woman followed by the shark and kept my arms and legs tucked. I'd never know how many night creatures were scenting out my tender flesh.

The engine became louder. It was closer. I wondered if they'd seen me in the distance and knew where I was. I heard the motor louder and then fading. They were circling. If they knew anything about diving, they'd know I couldn't stay down much longer.

The engine stopped. It was a bad sign. With my luck they'd drop anchor right on my head. I couldn't hear anything but my bubbles. Did that mean they were far off? I had no idea if an anchor hitting sand could be heard for any distance. Was it like a tree falling in the woods? If nobody heard it, was there a sound? Was there an anchor? I was losing it.

I exhaled slowly trying to calm down. I thought about my bubbles. If those guys were anywhere close they'd see the rolling circles breaking on the surface. They would know exactly where I was. They could be sitting above me, watching my breath, knowing that every bubble was part of the countdown and they were in total control of the situation.

I thought of leaving the package and swimming as far as I could get. I could swim and float in the warm water. It sounded better than sitting there. Enzo wasn't coming back for me. But where to go? Would they follow my bubbles or stay with the drugs? There was a good possibility I could escape if I had the guts to take control. I thought about what I had – a little air, some lift bags, a knife. Enough drugs, whatever kind, for a cruise ship. So what?

I felt the line from the center of the trap. Fuck. The float was bobbing on the surface. If only I would have thought to cut it off. That finalized it. They were surely anchored, keeping an eye on the float and my bubbles. I had to get away from there before they sent somebody down.

I thought I could feel a slight current pulling the float line right so my bubbles should be going up at an angle in that direction. Whatever it was, I wanted to head opposite.

I unbuckled my vest and let it slip down onto the trap next to me. I kept the regulator in my mouth while I untied one of the partially filled bags from the corner and wrapped the line around my wrist. It was just enough to keep me off the bottom. I unstrapped my knife and grabbed the lobster ball line and cut it. I hoped those guys would be confused when the float drifted away. At least they had to stay anchored to keep track of their prize.

Next I took off a glove and tucked it under my arm while I put a little more air in the lift bag with my regulator. I could feel myself working up a panic and I stopped. I took a big breath and let it out slowly, feeling it rattle through my trachea as I tried to calm my trembling. I went through it again and I wasn't any better.

I took another gulp and started to move fast. I pulled the regulator out of my mouth. It was worse than breaking off a last kiss. By feel, I tucked a finger of the glove into the button to make it freeflow slightly. I kept my weight belt on so I wouldn't risk rising up with full lungs and killing myself with a bubble to the brain. I picked and finned my way across the sand without one glove, holding my breath and hoping not to grab a stingray, or sea urchin, or worst of all a stonefish. I got as far as I could before I dared to exhale and take a breath off the dump valve in the top of the bag. I lost a lot of air trying to suck off the flat surface. I hoped I was far enough. My lungs were burning, but I got a breath.

I moved slow, sucking off the bag and hoping they were still watching my regulator bubbles and hadn't figured out I'd left it. When the bag ran out I would have to swim to the surface exhaling rapidly enough not to burst my lungs, but slowly enough to make it without running out of breath – just like in class, but without a regulator inches from my lips.

I ran right into something. It cut into my shoulder and almost caused me to spill the quarter bag of air I had left. It was a taut line. I took a sip of air and followed the chain across the sand, finally reaching the hard prongs. I'd bumped into their anchor rode. They had a lot of scope and were still sitting downcurrent guarding my bubbles.

With the current taking away all the effort, I picked my way along the chain to the line. I took a tiny sip of air and unsnapped the knife from my calf. I would have smiled if my lips weren't mashed so tight in fear. I used the serrated edge and felt it slice through. With a little luck maybe they wouldn't notice until they'd drifted a ways. I took another slurp of air and finned ahead as fast as I could. I didn't know what the distance was between us, but every foot gave me a better chance to hide in the dark.

In a few yards I ran out on that breath. I dropped the weight belt and stuck my face over the bag to get my last good lung-full of air and pushed up. I made my mouth into a small O as I'd been taught. The dead silence was broken by the pitiful whine of my vocal cords as I let out my slow stream of bubbles. I wanted to blast, but I made my legs move moderately, in a rhythmic compact motion. I couldn't see a thing. Couldn't tell if I was headed upward. It seemed to take forever.

I thought about fish in tanks and how they would swim upside down if you put the light source on the bottom. I thought of skiers digging themselves deeper into avalanches. I had my arms above my head, the knife in my hand, and for all I knew I might be spiraling back down in an arch like a rocket. Any second I might spear myself into the sand and die.

Seconds passed and I was still finning. My lungs ached. I'd let out too much air too soon. How did I ever expect to make it?

I finned in panic waiting for the involuntary intake of water that would finish me. I made a rush, a boost that shot my head into the air. I gasped a breath and it burned like hell, and I took in another one on top of it. I exhaled and grabbed a third, waiting for a bubble from my swift ascent to reach my brain and put me out. But I was lucky, no instant death, yet.

I pushed my mask down around my neck and did a slow three-sixty turn. I didn't see anything. Then I spotted them off a short distance, silhouetted against a sky that was just barely lighter than they were – two men standing in a low boat looking over the side. The boat seemed too small for a drug boat.

I licked the salt on my lips and enjoyed another breath – really enjoyed it. It was tinged with marijuana. These guys weren't professional drug dealers, maybe bone fishing guides playing a lucky guess, just drifting into dawn getting high. My tank must have run out by then. With no point of reference they might not even realize they were moving.

I breast-stroked quietly to put more distance between us. I didn't think they'd spot me until the sun came up, but I wondered if they'd radioed friends to help. Why else would they be sitting there. I tried to distinguish an island somewhere or a rock, but there was nothing but water for miles. I floated to rest a while. The men were still in view. I wondered when Enzo would come back for the package. I skulled and floated and began to shiver.

With the first glow of dawn I heard a sound. It was a low purr, an engine way off. It was too smooth and loud to be Enzo. I thought shit – the Bahamians' pals.

I pushed my mask over my eyes and put my snorkel into my mouth. The purr turned into a roar. A black cigarette boat with twin engines cut across the horizon. It turned and the first sunrays caught a wishbone of water under the point of the hull. Three people stood in the cockpit.

My hopes drained.

The cigarette didn't turn my way. It headed for the small boat. One of the Bahamians grabbed the engine cord and whipped it, but nothing happened. He turned back to try again.

Backfire added to the rumble. The cigarette cut its engine and curved into a spraying stop beside the small boat. They lined up parallel. That's when I saw one Bahamian slumped over the side. The other was out of sight.

I felt all the blood rush to my head. They were dead. I

visualized the man in the bottom of the boat in his puddle of blood, a tiny puddle inside this big one where I was floating – and the fellow with his brains dripping into the water with me.

One of the men from the cigarette climbed over the side of the fishing boat. He slipped the dangling man into the water and then reached down and dragged the other one over the side. I heard the splash.

The twin engines started up again. This time the guy aimed downward and I heard what I'd learned were not backfires. The smaller boat began to sink.

The cigarette moved slowly toward me about a third of the way and stopped. It was idling and I saw the three men, standing, waiting. I didn't have a chance.

I squinted. One of them had his elbows bent in a position up to his face and I guessed he was scanning with binoculars, looking for that red float.

He put down his arms and pointed and I knew I was spotted. There was nowhere to go. The cigarette took on power and glided over the water towards me. As it got closer I saw a black man and Blondie. There was Enzo in the stern. Blood started to flow in my legs again. He must have gotten the captain and found a local to bring them back. I froze. The relief emptied out of me. It was either Enzo or Blondie who had murdered the two fishermen.

I didn't have time to think about it. They were beside me. Enzo smiled down and I felt a smile flash on my face in spite of everything – I was going to live.

The sun was shining in Enzo's black hair and catching the mist on his arms as he helped me up the ladder and wrapped a towel around me. It was warm. I was weak. I let him hold me and kiss me while the captain stood staring at my face. I closed my eyes.

"Okay," Blondie said. "We're short on time here. Tell us what happened to the package, babe."

I jerked my head up and Enzo moved to the side. I caught fire. I was boiling over, even with the fear. "I guess it's still there, bub."

"Still where?" Enzo asked.

"Still where it was. Close anyway." I looked at Blondie. "Enzo and I were on anchor when we brought it up. I only drifted a few seconds before I let it back down." I pointed at Enzo. "When he took off."

Blondie stuck out his hand and Enzo passed him the GPS. He punched in the numbers and got a heading. The Bahamian gunned the twin engines.

"I had to get help," Enzo whispered. "Nothing I could do."

I didn't say anything. In seconds we reached the spot and banked down. Enzo started to gear up. They had a whole pile of dive gear and I thought, shit, what couldn't you get in a jiffy when you had money. I reached into the pile to grab a vest.

Enzo put his hand on my arm. He called to Blondie. "Mona can't go down now," he said. "She's been in the water for hours."

I looked at Enzo in wonder. I glanced at Blondie. His face was set in a sneer. "Hell if I'm staying up here with him," I said. "I've had a long surface interval waiting for you. Just give me a gulp of something – whatever you have – and I'll be set."

Enzo cocked his head and frowned. I thought he was pleased and maybe relieved. He pulled out a gallon of water, and I drank about a quarter of it. My arms were shaky and I kept trying to put the picture together to know if Enzo was the one who shot the Bahamians. I don't know why. It was only a matter of who happened to be holding the gun. Enzo was just as cool as the captain. A couple of murders weren't going to ruin his day.

My life was completely fucked and there wasn't anything I could do about it by then. I picked out a regulator, vest, and tank and got ready to head down. I thought about my gear at the bottom, partially paid off on my credit card. Maybe I could recover it. What did it really matter? I was past recovery myself.

Blondie punched the numbers on the GPS and we swung over there in seconds.

Enzo slipped into the water and went down while I finished gearing up. I didn't care whether we found the drugs or not. I wondered if they'd kill me if we didn't.

Enzo popped his head up as I was ready to step over the side.

He pulled his regulator out. "It's right here. You did it, woman. You saved our fortune. Nobody could have done better."

He squeezed my arm as I climbed overboard, then motioned to the boat that we were headed down.

"Move it fast," the captain yelled. "It's getting light."

"Follow our bubbles," Enzo yelled. "It's less than twenty yards west."

I stuck the unfamiliar regulator in my mouth and ducked down. I followed Enzo as he followed a heading he'd taken on his compass. He grinned back at me through his regulator when he spotted the package. By saving the drugs, I'd done something he could respect. I felt it. I was nauseous and it didn't have anything to do with the motion of the water.

There it sat, resting like a comfortable seat the way I'd left it. The three empty floats were still attached and my dive tank and vest lay on its back beside it. Enzo had more float bags and he attached one. I filled the others.

The trap started to lift and I motioned that I was going to stay down. I pointed to his lift bags and he handed one over. I couldn't leave my gear behind. It was nearly new. I turned off the valve even though the tank must have been filled with water. It took me a few minutes to tie on the lift bag and fill it enough to make it rise off the bottom. I checked over everything. I was really just screwing around down there. It was a place where I knew the rules and I didn't want to leave. Crazy. My time was running out one way or another.

I hugged my gear and finned up. Enzo was waiting, watching over the side.

"I was just getting ready to head back down," he said. "I told the captain you were getting your gear. The asshole," he said more quietly. He put out those dark shining arms and I handed over my stuff.

I looked forward and there was Blondie, staring and smouldering, the handgun stuck in his belt. A kind of thrill ran through me. I bet I'd surprised the hell out of him by staying alive.

They'd already stashed the booty in the bags and coolers on board while I was down. I still didn't know for sure what it was.

I was barely in the boat when the captain hollered to the Bahamian to take off.

"Fuck you, man," Enzo yelled.

The captain didn't say a word.

The Bahamian started off slowly and I made it to a seat. I let Enzo wrap me up again. It felt good. I went for the tenderness regardless of knowing the ruthless bastard that he was. He rubbed me dry and then blotted my suit. I saw Blondie watching and shifted the angle so my back was to him.

"How come I'm always having to dry you off and warm you up?" Enzo asked me. He worked his way down and felt the hard cyalume, still in the crotch of my bikini where I'd put it. "What the fuck's this?" He pressed it against me. "You got your own ying-yang now?"

I reached in and pulled it out, handed it to him. The green glow was gone. "Yeah. I've always wanted one of my own," I said. It didn't come out funny like I wanted. I was past humor. I thought, fuck, if I did have a dick, maybe I wouldn't be where I was right now. I could choose my own kind of trouble.

He started drying my hair and I let myself sink back against his chest. "So what was in the package? Cocaine?"

"Black tar from Mexico."

"Tar?" I sat up.

"Heroin. A fortune's worth."

I felt a knife go through my chest. It was fear and shame. All the life drained out of me and I slunk against Enzo again and held on. He kissed my head and cuddled close. There was something so sweet and unexpected in him – and he was a murderer.

24

◆◆◆◆◆◆◆◆◆◆◆◆◆◆◆◆◆

I didn't want to stay at my apartment when we got home, and I couldn't face going back to the hospital. Both places were hostile to me, too real. I wanted to be with Enzo. He said it would be fine for me to stay there.

I called in and told the nurse manager I had problems that were going to keep me out for a while. She was more sympathetic than I deserved and told me I could probably work a graveyard shift when I was ready. I wanted to say I'd almost worked it permanently, but of course, I couldn't tell her anything. Now Enzo was the only person I could trust.

The next day I stopped at my place to feed the animals and get some clothes. The beautiful cage Ivan's friend had built was against the window. It was about six feet high, five feet long, perfect for Ignats. He could sun through the wire part on top and sleep in the glass enclosure on the bottom if it got cool. Ivan had rearranged the furniture to make the cage fit and managed to get Ignats inside. I had to remember to thank him and give him the money for his friend.

Ig scrambled over to the door of the cage when I brought his food. I had to put my hand above him to make sure he didn't jump out when I swung open the door.

He seemed more friendly, but I didn't have time for him. I felt nervous. I tripped over Snickers when she came out to rub on my calves. I dodged kittens everywhere I moved. I had a lot of cats and they'd grown. I petted them as quickly as I could – there were so many. I felt like I had to dash back over to Enzo's before something changed. I wasn't sure what.

I left a note on Ivan's door saying thanks and telling him he was off feeding duty. I had to run.

I was due for my steroids and some maxed-out lifting, so when Enzo went to the shop I got over to the gym. I had three thousand dollars in my bag and I figured it had to be at least double the price of the cycles I needed. I decided to ask Rory for the rest of my first cycle and then one other in case it took time for me to make new connections. I'd tell him I had to change gyms. I would be throwing away a lot of money, but that didn't matter now. I had to break off the sex routine before Enzo caught on. The severity of that situation had lodged in my stomach.

Rory was doing his squats when I walked in. It was after five and there were quite a few guys and a couple of women around the room. They were all big. I looked closely at the women. I wondered if they were both fucking him to get their stuff. Pretty busy life he had.

A spotter was helping Rory to do a few last reps, pushing the edge. Rory's face was blood red and his neck a mass of veins and muscles stretching under the tight sheath of skin. He set up the bar.

"Hey, Rory," I said. "I need to talk a minute, when you get the chance."

He smiled in between deep breaths. "One last set."

He added another ten pounds and I watched while he finished. He used everything he had, and then did twelve more, with the spotter only helping him put the bar up. I wondered how he knew his limits so perfectly, something I needed to learn.

He toweled off and the other guy did the same and left. Rory and I walked over to the desk.

I spoke low. "I need the rest of my cycle and the next one." I gave him a story about moving.

He didn't look like he would go for it. I opened my purse

so he could see the stack of hundreds. "I'll pay extra for your trouble."

His eyes brightened a little. He leaned over the desk and looked down between my thighs. "How much?"

I glared. "Three times your cost."

"Maybe," he said. "I'll be here early tomorrow. Come then. We'll see what we can do."

I knew *early* meant I was going to have to fuck him if I wanted to complete the transaction. Okay. One last time wouldn't kill me. By that point, I wasn't very worried about death.

The next day Enzo had a morning dive with a class, so he was gone by eight. I was out the door two minutes later. I raced over to my apartment and fed the animals. Rory opened at nine and if nobody was there I could get in and out.

I passed Ivan pulling out of the apartment lot and he stopped, but I waved and kept on going to my parking place. I wanted to give him the cage money, but I didn't have time to talk. I noticed the wind had picked up as I got out of the car. There were dark clouds coming and I felt a burst of energy with the cool air behind me.

When I opened the door, four cats were draped across the couch, a couple on the windowsill. They looked at me with interest, but I rushed into the kitchen and filled their bowls and grated up a tiny piece of squash for Ignats. It wasn't his usual portion, but it was all I had. Details were starting to get me down.

Ignats was sleeping on the corner shelf in his cage and I set the food in front of him. I didn't have time to hold his dish while he ate. I went into the bedroom and grabbed more shorts and shirts to take to Enzo's.

On my way out I glanced at the cats again and Snickers turned towards me. Her ears were down. "Be good kitties," I said. "See you tomorrow." I hadn't named the new ones.

Rory was unlocking the door when I got to the gym. I walked up beside him. "Got my stuff?"

"You got mine?"

"You bet." I reached into my bag to show him the edges of the bills in an envelope.

He grinned and stuck his finger in my waistband. His teeth gleamed against his smooth tan. He was carrying a sky-blue nylon bag over his shoulder that brought out his eyes. I followed him inside just as the rain came down. I handed him the money and he counted it and nested it in a towel in his bag.

I went ahead to his favorite bench and started taking off my clothes. I just wanted to finish it. I flung my leotard across the bar and hung the bra over the end. Rory walked toward me from his office. I faced him and straddled the bench. I was conscious of my clitoris, a tight feeling gathering there. My clit had begun to grow a little, one of the side effects Rory had told me about. I inspected it, rolled it between my fingers. My own little penis, sturdy and sensitive.

Rory came up and set a plastic bag on the floor. "This is the rest – your other cycle."

"Great," I said. I bent forward while he swabbed the site with an alcohol pad and stuck me. I didn't even tense. I thought I could feel the vitamin S running through me, my muscles thickening and strengthening. It ran straight down into my tiny taut organ.

"You like that, huh?" Rory said. "You got your own pecker, so now you don't need anybody else." He was smiling wide. "All you women like it," he said, "till you have to start taping it down."

I smelled his sweat and the scent of aloe when he climbed on top of me. In a few seconds I had my mouth on his and I was arching hard against him, rutting in a momentum equal to his. It was powerful, the last time. Warm waves ran over my chest and forced an animal sound from my lungs. Rory groaned and stopped. Lightning flashed and we both jumped. We laughed, panted for air, and laughed again.

He stared down at me. "You're hitting the top on those roids," he said. "Pretty soon, you'll lose interest in sex."

I couldn't believe it the way I felt, and not with Enzo around. I wasn't ready to worry about it. I just wanted to get out of there.

He swung over to the floor and I scooted and picked my bottoms off the bar and stepped into them and pulled on my bra. I was sweaty, cool, and relieved. I sat down to put my shoes on.

My little bag of goodies was beside me. I would crank on my workout and then never come back to that fucking gym again.

I heard the squeak of the door and the steady downpour outside. A shock of heat went through me. Rory had forgotten to lock.

I straightened my top and glanced over at him. He had his shirt on and was adjusting his shorts. I looked back at the door. A guy in rain gear and a hood had stepped inside, dripping. He closed the door and it banged. He flipped back the hood. It was Enzo. My stomach lurched. He smiled. I finished tying my shoe and stood up. I couldn't see his face well enough to tell anything.

"Hey, babe," he hollered.

I breathed.

He walked slowly over. "Dive's cancelled. Bad storm."

I wondered if I needed to wipe my mouth or straighten my hair. I was afraid to. "Oh, too bad, huh?" I said. I couldn't believe I hadn't realized about the weather.

"Not so bad. I drove by and saw your car. Thought maybe you'd want to have breakfast. Are you done?"

"Yeah," I said. I was still catching my breath. I hadn't lifted the bar even once, but I grabbed my towel and bag.

"Looks like you've really been goin' at it," he said. "You're all flushed."

"Yeah." I stared into his eyes. I thought he was playing with me before he went for the jugular.

He stared back. "The rain will cool you off," he said. He reached over my shoulder and pulled my ponytail. I thought it felt a little rough, but I started walking ahead, past Rory who was digging in a drawer at the desk. I watched his face.

"Catch ya later, Ror," Enzo called.

"Yeah, man," Rory mumbled.

I nearly dived out the door into the cool rain. I thought a cloud of steam might form above my head with the heat I was putting off. I kept expecting Enzo to drop the bomb in the car, but he didn't. I must have been saved by seconds.

25

◆◆◆◆◆◆◆◆◆◆◆◆◆◆◆◆

Over the next few weeks I moved all my clothes into Enzo's house, but I had a lease and needed my apartment for the animals and storage. Each morning while Enzo was still sleeping, I went over to feed them. I knew they were lonesome, but Enzo didn't want pets, so it was the only choice temporarily.

Enzo had given me ten thousand on the dive, and I'd paid off all my debts and found a new gym. He convinced me I didn't need to keep my nursing job. He said the piddling salary wasn't worth my time. I was happy to quit. I felt out of place at the hospital, a hypocrite. I couldn't fool myself about the lost lives I was contributing to with drug trafficking.

Enzo had plenty of money for me and the household, and without a job I could spend my days working out and playing with him when he was home. I knew he had other jobs coming up in the future, but I didn't want to think about it. If he asked me to help, I planned to say no. He could easily find another diver.

I tried to convince myself that Enzo never meant to leave me in the ocean to die – that his only choice was to go for help – but I couldn't. It would have taken only seconds to drop the box and help me into the dinghy. I learned to live with it. I told myself that he had reacted out of fear. Besides, it was all in the past, and he felt different about me now that I had come through for him.

He told me he was proud how I risked my life and managed to save the profits – he loved me for that. I didn't deal with the idea of his being a murderer. I hadn't seen him fire any shots. Blondie was the one.

Enzo had other jobs going on all the time, but he didn't give me the details. Once in a while he went out after two a.m. and came back in the morning. He said not to worry. I didn't ask any questions.

In the next two months my workouts were the only part of my life I had any interest in, besides Enzo. I was spending up to five hours a day in the gym, working upper, lower, and cardial, and the rest of my time eating chicken and tuna. I always took a late afternoon nap. I was halfway through my second cycle, had gained fifteen pounds of solid muscle, lost all traces of adipose tissue. I was cut. My vascular system had started to show. I tanned to keep an even golden tone. It wasn't the adventurous life I'd imagined I wanted, but creating myself – with Enzo's help – was fulfilling.

My clitoris was growing up to be the pet of the household – the only kind of pet Enzo could tolerate. It had grown to three beautiful, smooth inches, sensitive as any penis, and it hardened when I fingered it. Enzo had named it Tiny.

I had less appetite for sex, like Rory had said, but it wasn't important. I would get it back. For Enzo, it meant he didn't have to spend time on my pleasure and he could concentrate on his preference. I learned to relax so the physical pain had lessened, but I never enjoyed the feeling, although I made Enzo believe I did.

I couldn't deny that our relationship was pathological. My autonomy was shot. But I didn't care. I'd grown to accept Enzo as a predatory machine in every part of his existence. He was a true loner, with no conscience, and the nature to get whatever he wanted. He wanted a lot. Without a concrete reason, I knew I was only the flavor of the moment, and he would move on. Of course, the risk made me want him more. I hated him and his power over me, yet I admired and worshipped every monstrous, evil molecule of him.

One night after he'd finished with me, I lay on my back recovering from the sting of his knife-like penetration. He was snoring. I began rolling Tiny between my thumb and forefinger, feeling chills run up it. The color was a purply fuchsia and it nearly glowed under the lamp. I was perfect, self-contained. I dragged my mind for the reason I needed Enzo so desperately.

He propped his head up and opened his eyes. "Still playing with that thing?" He moved over and cupped his hand on it, tucked it into my vagina, and kept it there with his finger.

I twitched it and he smiled. "How much bigger do you think it's gonna get?"

"I don't know," I said. "I'm not finished with this cycle and I'd planned to do another one."

"I have an idea."

"Don't tell me to stop. I haven't reached my goal."

"No. I was thinking that you're out of balance. Your tits are gone and you're growing a prick." He reached up and brushed across my flat chest.

He was right. My chest was like a twelve-year-old's, with a little extra skin. Even my nipples were smaller.

"I thought maybe you'd want to fill out up top – like you were."

"Implants?" The idea made me shudder.

"Yeah. I'll pay for 'em. You'll have it all. You'll be perfect."

"I don't know." I couldn't ignore the health factor. I was already maxed out on roids. I wondered how many odds I could stack against me. "They wouldn't be real."

"You call this real?" He flicked Tiny with his finger.

It stung, but I didn't let on.

"Go for it." He ran his fingers over my chest and down my sternum. "For me."

I felt a threat in it. He wanted me to get them. There was no thought beyond that. "They could turn hard from the scar tissue."

"What's wrong with hard? The harder the better." He motioned to my body with a jerk of his chin. "Isn't that right?"

"Yeah," I said.

I found a plastic surgeon and made the appointment for

surgery in the gap between my steroid cycles. The nurse said it would be two months until I could do any heavy lifting, but I knew I could cut it down to a few weeks. I was a fast healer. I realized I would be a total recreation of myself with those additions, and I began to look forward to my new parts and the attention Enzo would give me.

The three days after the operation were only uncomfortable. I was used to suffering – no pain, no gain. I packed myself into a tight bra to reduce swelling and lay around on the couch watching soaps and skimming a catalogue from Victoria's Secret. Enzo had brought it. He wanted me to order some slinky stuff. I'd never worn lacy lingerie, but I could start.

I wasn't allowed a shower, or even a hot bath, because it would increase circulation. I started thinking of how many weeks it had been since I'd been out of the water. I tried to let my mind sink into the blue like I used to, but the swim through blackness was all I could remember and the bodies we left back there. I didn't have the joy and wonder inside me anymore.

By the end of the week of surgery, the ache in my chest was no worse than another sore muscle. I was back to the gym in two more weeks working my lower body and feeling great. I saw some of the regulars staring at my new chest, and I stuck it out. Those babies were D cups. Enzo had helped find the true me.

My sexual feelings were gone, but I didn't need them. Sex was another workout. I felt Enzo's renewed interest. He enjoyed strutting around with my body.

One Friday night I got the idea for us to stop in at Seabirds. I hadn't been there or to the shop since the trip to the Bahamas. I had some idea of seeing the diver crowd again, trying to get back to the purity of the ocean. Enzo said he didn't mind stopping by. He still went regularly after his classes.

When we walked in, the fishy smell took me back to my first days of diving, the excitement I used to feel listening to the stories and dreaming. It made me know the absence of those feelings in my present life.

I recognized a diving crowd from the T-shirt styles and sun-bleached hair. There was some kind of relaxed look after being down, or maybe it was what I imagined seeing. We sat at the bar and each ordered a beer. I looked around to see if anybody I knew was hanging out – Dennis or Charlie. I thought of the blind pervert – Steve – wondered if he was still diving. The night of the party seemed years in the past.

The crowd had changed – a bunch of geeks. I had no interest in anybody but Enzo. I put my hand on his thigh, stroked it lightly, smoothing the hairs straight with my fingers. I'd be ready to go home after one beer.

A slender, dark-haired woman appeared at his shoulder between us. She had chocolate eyes and long lashes. Her heavy gold earrings caught the light. Even from the side I could tell she was gorgeous.

"Hello there," Enzo said.

I didn't like the deep tone I heard in his voice.

The woman smiled. Her teeth were perfect and white between soft red lips. "It's good you get away from that shop once in a while."

It was a silly line. Enzo didn't spend much time in the shop.

"What are you up to?" Enzo asked. "Got your homework finished?"

"I have a couple questions for you," she said. She looked at me. "But they can wait."

"This is Ramona," Enzo said.

"Ramona, this is Elisa, one of my students in the advanced class."

"Hi," I said.

She nodded. She turned back to Enzo. "I'll see you Tuesday then. I was just leaving." She brushed his hair and shoulder with her hand as she turned.

"Yeah. See you," he said.

She flashed a big smile.

I watched Enzo's eyes follow her out the door. It was like he forgot about me sitting there.

"One of your students?" I said.

"Yeah. Is there a problem?"

"Nope." Her attitude was clear to me and I didn't like it. But

I had no concrete basis to say anything, and I didn't want to light his fuse.

We stayed another hour without seeing anybody. Then Charlie came in. An older woman dressed in a suit was in front of him. They seemed to be together.

Enzo motioned them over.

Charlie didn't look happy, but he spoke to the woman and they headed in our direction. He glanced at me and his eyes opened up. I don't think he recognized me at first. He pointed out two seats next to Enzo and they sat down. The woman was pretty in a delicate, businesslike way, every hair perfect.

"Have you met my wife?" Charlie asked Enzo. "Jenny – Ramona and Enzo."

She put out her hand to each of us and said she'd just gotten off work at the bank, the reason for wearing the suit.

We all talked for a while, but the dive talk wasn't lively enough to keep my attention. I focused on Charlie. He looked happier than before. It was fine with me. So they'd never gotten the divorce. It made sense for Jenny to be his wife.

I pictured Elisa on the boat in her bathing suit. She couldn't compete with my muscularity, but she didn't need to. I pictured her with Enzo.

26

◆◆◆◆◆◆◆◆◆◆◆◆◆◆◆◆

All weekend the beautiful Elisa lurked in my head. By Tuesday I had the scenario clear. I knew Enzo was going to come home late from the shop that night, even if he didn't know it yet. She was offering and he wouldn't pass her up. It was against his nature.

He knew I'd take it too, along with anything else he dished out. Love was pain. I'd learned it. The lover submits and the other inflicts – without even trying.

I thought of going to Seabirds that night. I hadn't been out by myself since Enzo "swept me off my feet" at the party. I considered calling Dennis to meet for a drink. He was nice. He'd be happy to see me – maybe. Maybe not. I wasn't the person he knew before. I could visit my pets, or Ivan, or Claire – I owed them all a visit. I hadn't seen Claire since Spike's death. I decided to stay home in the gloom, counting minutes and hoping to be wrong about Enzo.

The suspense was overpowering. I couldn't watch TV. I tried tricks I'd played as a kid, holding my breath and guessing how many times I could walk around the room. If I was right Enzo would come home. I guessed ten and it was impossible. The tension sped up my oxygen consumption. I guessed six and made it, but could I count the second try? By ten-thirty I knew Enzo had followed through. I lay there on the couch, catatonic and sweating until I fell asleep.

He got home around three, clomped in and shut the door. I raised my head and looked at his sleepy eyes. He'd just crawled out of Elisa's bed. I wondered how many times he had come between ten and three. It was a guessing game without reward.

"Still up?"

I didn't answer.

"Guess so," he said. He started to move and I thought he was going to leave me as stiff as a dead mackerel and go in to bed.

"How was it?" I asked. I bit the inside of my lower lip.

He looked into my eyes. "I'm sorry I didn't tell you I'd be late. I didn't know."

My throat ached. I was shaking.

"Is that all?" I asked him. "You're just casually sleeping around? Am I going insane?" I stood up in his face.

"Fuck! Why are you so upset? We're not married."

I could see his color intensifying. He was breathing hard. He was ready to take control – his easy defense.

"No sense wasting time," he said. "It's late. We've been fine – without any fucking promises. I thought you wanted to be free to do your thing too."

"What thing?" I flinched.

"You can't force it. You're the same as me. Don't kid yourself."

I nodded.

"I hear Rory's left town," he said. He looked at me with his coolest eyes, then shrugged.

Everything went out of me. I didn't want to know any more about it, what kind of force had been applied there.

"We're the same, no?" Enzo said.

I shook my head. I had been like him, but I wasn't anymore. I knew that smothered feeling, and what I'd done to survive it. I knew Enzo would do exactly as he needed to make himself happy.

He sat down on the couch. "Don't sweat it. Like the saying – 'If something belongs to you, let it go and it'll come back.' You know?"

"Fuck the clichés." I slunk down onto the couch. I had no options if I wanted to stay.

He gave me a kiss on the top of the head and turned up my chin to look in my eyes. "It's just for spice," he said. "I wouldn't even want to see her more than once a week."

I thought of punching him in the kidney, rupturing something. He stood and walked into the bedroom. There wasn't anything I could do. He was on the way out.

I walked into the kitchen and hit the wall with my fist. It made a loud womp and caved in the plasterboard. My knuckles stung like hell. Fuck. I slumped against the damage and slid down to the floor.

I sat there on the cold tile for a while, burning up, then went to his bed. I pulled the sheet over my head and turned my face into the pillow. There was the smell of his hair and neck in it. I gave myself up to him. After all, this crime was far less than murder.

He touched my neck under the sheet and I rolled against him. He shoved his tongue in my mouth and in a second I was up on my knees stripping off my nightie. I locked myself onto him and beat my pelvis into his. I was wild in my desperation. I shrieked with the pleasure in my vagina and cried with the pain in my chest. Tears flowed all the way through my orgasm, the first one in a long time.

The next Tuesday I decided to visit Claire while Enzo was gone. Something to keep my sanity. We'd talked on the phone once since Spike, and she didn't blame me. She was the only woman I felt anything in common with. I thought Claire might go with me to a new bar.

I drove over there with my mind on Enzo, and made a wrong turn. I knew it was going to be tough making it through the night, but I was tough.

I stopped to feed the animals first. I'd cut my visits to two mornings a week, so I knew the cats could use fresh water and a refill of dry food. The two litter pans would be overflowing. Ignats might eat.

When I opened the door they all ran. Even Snickers was

frightened for a minute seeing me at night. The rest of them wouldn't even come close. I filled the dish and watched them. They were almost like feral cats in their posture and the way they darted and hid. I resolved to come back more often.

Ignats was looking a little pale under the light in his cage. I noticed there was only one clump of hardened faeces on the wire bottom, instead of one for each day since I'd scraped it. I passed the bedroom on my way to the bathroom. I'd never taken off the sheets and they were hanging part on the floor from where the cats had run up and down. I could see hair and dirt from the doorway. I knew I should spend some time cleaning. It had been months.

I thought of the time Enzo had brought me home from the rescue and tucked me into the clean sheets. I felt the tinge of sadness when I remembered my innocence when we were first together, and thought how everything had changed, no going back.

I ran about six inches of warm water in the tub. I knew Ig needed to soak to relieve his constipation. I carried him into the bathroom and lowered him gently. He lunged at the side, but couldn't get out. He kept on doing it, scrabbling his feet on the slick enamel. I closed the bathroom door. I figured a half hour would be long enough.

I mixed his food and set the dish in the cage. I left everything and walked down to Claire's. I knocked on her door and waited, picturing Elisa in a desk with Enzo hovering over her. I knocked again. Claire opened the door.

"Hi, how's it going?" I said.

She looked.

I saw she didn't recognize me. "It's Ramona."

She blinked. "Oh. Sorry, I just woke up. I don't have my contacts in."

"I thought maybe you'd want to go somewhere for a drink," I said. It was hardly worth asking.

"Oh, I can't. I'm headed for central Florida tonight – to meet up with the circus."

"Wow," I said. "Are you a carney?"

"Bally girl," she said. "I sit outside the freak show with my snake. You know, make some ballyhoo to build a tip – lure the marks, that is."

"Oh." I wasn't sure what she meant. "Sounds like fun," I told her. For a split-second I wished I could go – till I thought about Enzo.

"Yeah. I take turns with the midget."

She'd gotten a new snake and named him Nail. "He's not as big as Spike," she said, "but he's friendlier."

I imagined her in a skimpy beaded costume with Nail wound around her waist, his head between her breasts, tail between her thighs.

"I'd show him to you, but I don't want to wake him."

I never heard of not waking a snake. "Well, good luck," I told her. I turned to go.

"By the way, Ramona," she said. "You need to check your animals. I've seen those cats on the windowsills, and they don't look real healthy."

I glanced back at her and I could tell she was trying to be nice about it. I knew my life was getting out of control. Now other people were noticing. "Will do," I said. "Thanks."

As I walked back to my apartment I noticed Ivan's place was dark. His car wasn't in its space. I figured next time I should plan ahead.

I went back to my apartment and checked Ignats. Sure enough, he'd moved his bowels and was looking chipper. I picked him up and let some water drain off before I held him against the towel on my chest to take him back to the cage. He went with me more easily than I remembered from ever before. I kissed him on the side of the head and set him on the shelf under his light. He looked at his food dish and started eating. He took it when he could get it now.

I thought I'd drive to Seabirds until I checked my watch. I didn't think Enzo would take Elisa there after class, but I wasn't sure. Might be a whole group of students with him. The last thing I wanted to do was run into them.

I went home and went to bed. I didn't turn off the light. I lay there staring at the overhead light fixture, noticing the specks through the translucent glass, dead bugs that I should clean out. It would have been good for me to get up, and take it apart, feel that I'd done something besides increase my blood pressure and the acid in my stomach. I didn't move. I lay there and imagined Enzo looking into Elisa's beautiful eyes.

He came home at three. I didn't say anything. I rolled against him and held on. I was shaking with the tears inside me. He patted my head and seconds later started snoring. I clung to him until I finally fell asleep.

When he woke up he told me we had a Bahamas trip planned for the weekend. I was stunned. It came to me that he expected me to say no. Then he could take Elisa. In seconds I relived the rumble of wake as he turned and sped off and left me the last time, but the memory was less painful than thinking of him and Elisa together.

Friday morning we took off, same as the first time. Even the group of divers didn't look much different. My stomach felt worse though. I alternated between worrying about getting caught and the phonecall Enzo made on Thursday night. I knew it was Elisa. I didn't listen. I didn't ask about it. I knew he must be saying some kind of goodbye for the weekend and that meant something – more than a fuck.

When we docked at Weech's I felt myself watching Enzo's eyes. It was ridiculous – like he was going to find some female single-hander who had sailed in horny and fling her on the bunk next to me. I was getting carried away with my jealousy.

Friday night we went to the Angler. I danced and tossed down those sweet yellow birds, even though I shouldn't have been drinking. I started seeing Enzo's face double in front of me. If only he dropped his pants and had two dicks to match, everything would be fine – one for me and one for Elisa. If I kept on drinking maybe he'd grow more – plenty of spares for all the women.

I woke up during the night hot and dizzy. The sweat was beading on my chest and pooling in my navel. We were rocking peacefully on the water. I started thinking how I'd already gone through the big test last time and passed. Now I was much stronger and tougher. I had more muscle than most men and this was another chance for me to show Enzo how he needed me.

Saturday morning I sat up a little hung over, but the adrenalin was already pumping when I hopped off the bunk. Those male hormones were waking up. I flexed and saw the hardness and blue veins under the thin fine skin of my arm.

I felt my clitoris with its sturdy new size, got excited. Enzo was still sleeping and I stood at the mirror behind the door and pulled my abdomen into a tight washboard and tensed my pecs to jut the implants forward in their perfect roundness. The cords of muscle were thick in my neck and my face was hard in a grimace. Some heavy work would be good for me. I was ready to get down to the bottom and hoist that load. I could handle the deal against whatever Enzo and Neptune came up with.

That night I watched without feeling as Blondie passed Enzo the hardware – his gun and the GPS. I looked at that piece of metal, thinking it was the only thing stronger than I was. I picked it up and Enzo's eyes got round. It felt light with my new strength. I put it back in his bag.

There was a couple enjoying the starry night on deck when it came time to go, so we wore our clothes and I took my purse as if we were headed to the Big Game Club for drinks. The gear and dry bag were stowed under the seats of the dinghy like the first time.

It was a night without a moon and the water was choppy for riding in the small boat. We were soaked as soon as we got out in the wind. We headed to Big Game and then doubled back on the far side of the cut. We didn't see anybody on the way. The location had been changed to some distance north of the last drop. I spotted the float again. It was rocking on that black water.

Enzo anchored and I put together my gear and slipped into the water to wait for him. I was ready to duck under when I saw a light to the east. It was only a flash for a second. Something reflecting. I took off my mask and stared. I could make out another boat. It wasn't a sailboat at anchor. I thought it could be a large dark cigarette boat.

"Enzo," I whispered. Somebody over there." I pointed. "Did the captain send us an escort?"

His head jerked around. "No, no escort. Definitely not."

"See it?"

"Yeah, I see. Somebody's got information." He slung his vest into the hull. "You just stay there in the water. In fact, you can go on down and get started. I'll check 'em out."

"No," I mouthed. I sent him a vicious sneer to strengthen my whisper. "What if this guy comes over? Uh uh. I'm not that stupid."

"Look, I don't know what's going to happen. Just get down there. Hold the line." He pointed and I grabbed the line under the float, not knowing what he wanted me to do. He reached down and slashed off the buoy above it.

"Don't lose the line. Follow it down." He put his arm on my shoulder to keep me from reaching the boat. I had to do what he told me. I let the air out of my vest and held the line and submerged, pulled myself about ten feet down. I waited. I heard the purr of the cigarette and then the rumble of Enzo's outboard. I waited, sure he left me, not wanting to believe this could be happening again.

Silence – then shots – came to my ears. I had to go up. I let go of the line and bobbed to the surface. The dinghy was there. Enzo slipped into the water next to me. His face glowed in the green of his cyalume.

"What the hell are you doing? Where's the line?" he yelled.

I pulled out my regulator. "Christ's sake, Enzo, I didn't know what happened. I came up to see if you were all right."

"Fuck. Let's go." He slapped the regulator in his mouth and went down. His light went on as he dropped. I hoped we hadn't drifted far from the package, for my sake.

I watched him. I could feel a coldness penetrating my lungs. It wasn't from the water. It came from the inside, like my heart was frozen. I took a look for the cigarette boat. It was hard to see. Finally I spotted it, drifting. I couldn't see anybody in it. I knew there was a dead body, lying in the hull or fallen overboard. I let the air out of my vest and dropped.

I drifted down, and Enzo landed next to the package a few yards ahead of me. When I hit bottom he handed me the light and grabbed a lift bag and started to fill it.

I stood there holding the light on his hands, staring at him, recognizing his seething temper at my slight hesitation.

I let some water into my mask and blew it back out to calm myself, but it didn't work. Burning pain was building inside my head. I couldn't deny who Enzo was. Nobody meant anything to him, except for what he could get. I'd handed him my fucking soul – there wasn't anything else to offer. It wouldn't be long till he rid himself of me. I pictured Elisa's exotic face, still innocent, and Enzo's grin moving in. "Mother-fucker," I exhaled through my regulator.

I hunched and slipped the knife off my calf. Enzo was bent over the package busy tying on a bag, his bubbles rising in a stream on the exhale. I held the light steady as I drifted closer. Anger broiled out of me at his calm, and a flash of adrenalin filled me with strength. I clipped the light to my vest and waited for his long exhale. I grabbed his regulator hose behind him and sawed with the serrated edge of the knife. My view dissolved into a curtain of deafening bubbles.

He pushed upright and I let my weight down on his shoulders. He jerked but couldn't knock me off. I cut completely through the hard rubber hose. The bubbles were thick and loud. He spit out his regulator and twisted and grabbed for mine, but I dodged. I got his arms and pinned them to his sides. My arms were steel, my tits were rock pressed into his gut. I pinned him in a hard embrace against the drug trap. A wall of noise surrounded us. Nobody would have him – just the fish.

I felt the last struggle in him. He was writhing against me, using brute strength on his last half breath, but I was the stronger brute. I had my heels planted on his fins, my chin hard into his chest. I held on for my life. The light was wedged toward his face and I bent my neck back and peered through his mask at his wild black eyes. I'd never seen those eyes before, the black look in them, his real eyes.

His head slumped on my shoulder. I didn't stop moving. It

was too late to worry. I flattened him on his stomach on the box. There was enough line on the package to tie him to it.

I figured he just had to stay down till I hopped a sea plane out of Bimini in the morning. All I had to do was hide for the night. I had dry clothes and my purse in the dinghy. It would be an easier wait than the last time.

I didn't think Blondie would worry much about Enzo, except to keep it quiet. They'd have their loot when they found the body. The last thing Blondie would want was to get stuck in Bimini for an investigation. I just had to stay out of his way.

When I finished, Enzo was tied face down over the box, one limb to each corner like an "X marks the spot" on his treasure. I felt the strength in my legs as I kicked to the surface.

27

◆◆◆◆◆◆◆◆◆◆◆◆◆◆◆◆◆

I climbed into the dinghy and pulled the anchor. The glow from Bimini was easy to follow. I cut the engine at the inlet and paddled into the little canal that ran behind the unfinished condos. There were a few houses there, but most looked deserted. I tied up to a tree and put on my shorts and top and covered with a towel to wait the night out. I could hear the whining mosquitoes, but I couldn't tell if they bit, I was so fired up. I just lay there flat on my back until dawn, watching the sky and feeling my heart pump.

I thought about Blondie and his crew discovering Enzo. I figured they could find the package again. They'd probably heave Enzo aside to bring the trap up and get their shit on board. Maybe they'd cut him up into little pieces and chum the area. No body, less questions to answer.

I didn't care what happened anymore. I was moving with the instinct of survival, trying to make it back to my apartment with my animals, never to come out again.

Before dawn I paddled across the channel to the point. I felt safe in the quiet blackness. I set the dinghy adrift on the outgoing tide, just to be sure the police wouldn't find it, at least till I was gone. I sat on the side of the Chalk's terminal until it opened. Nobody passed by. I charged the first flight out on my Visa. I was easy to trace, but I hoped Blondie would be too busy hauling up his fortune in heroin to care about me.

I took a taxi from the airport and got to the apartment by ten. Everything was quiet when I turned the key. I felt spooked. It didn't seem right that I was home, and everything could go back to normal. I knew better.

I opened the door and smelled cat urine and mildew. My poor animals didn't deserve anything I'd done to them, and yet they wouldn't hate me. A few cats woke and stretched. They looked rumpled and scrawny, but I knew I could make them love me, despite the lonely, half-starved lives I'd given them.

I didn't see Ignats. I'd left him loose in the apartment. He was the smart one, like Enzo, never had any feeling at all for me, regardless of what I did. Life was fucked. Love was fucked.

I stepped inside. Cats stared from sills and couches. I walked up slowly and stroked them one by one, the length of their bodies and up their tails, poor nameless children. Snickers glanced up from her spot on the table and then put her head back down.

I looked around the room. It was the same disgusting mess I'd left it. No elves had come to my rescue. This time I had to start cleaning. Cat litter was everywhere. I hadn't changed the boxes for so long, I knew there'd be places they'd picked to take a clean shit. You couldn't change a cat from its natural good habits.

I dropped my gear bag and went into the bedroom to get the laundry basket. I grabbed dirty uniforms I'd flung on chairs and stripped the bed of its grimy cat-pawed sheets. There was something greenish-orange and slimy that I balled into the middle. I found five quarters and some bleach and detergent and hoisted the stinking basketful on my hip down to the laundry room.

Ivan was there taking his boxers from the dryer and folding them neatly in a pile. I felt a warmth run through me.

"Ivan," I said. "Hey." I set my basket down and went toward him, thinking to get a hug.

He turned his side to me and concentrated on the folding.

I stopped. I stared at his face but he didn't look up. My first thought was that he knew something about what I'd done – the

police had been there. Or he saw how I'd left the animals. Then
I pulled the truth out from somewhere in my tangled guts. I'd just
plain ignored him for weeks. I still owed him money and hadn't
even spoken to him since he'd provided the cage for Ignats.
Nothing had registered in my brain, I'd been so tied up with Enzo.
It was a fucking sacrifice I'd made for mindless passion.

I didn't say anything else. I didn't have the nerve to try to talk
him into being my friend again. I'd learned my limitations.

I turned and put the coins into the washer and let it fill part
way to add the bleach. I could see Ivan off to my side, folding his
boxers precisely. For a minute I felt detached, like I did from the
rest of my life, from the rest of the world. Then I started to become
angry – he was so calmly and purposely ignoring me. It was my
fault, but he could have given me a chance. It was all perfectly
understandable. I punched the whites down into the washer and
got out of there. It was obvious that even the simplest bond
produced an injury.

I jerked open my apartment door, dropped the basket, and
went into the kitchen. The water pans were nearly empty, crusty
around the edges with soggy food on the bottom. No dry food in
the bowls. The counter tops had dirty footprints and fur and
streaks of roach droppings. A glob of dried monkey biscuit
and squash was moulded over in the sink where I'd dumped and
left it. Garbage in the bin smelled like compost. Everything was
rotten.

I knew I had to make the place liveable again, but I couldn't
think why. I didn't have anything to live for, if I managed to stay
alive. Even the ocean had lost its fascination. I'd become a predator, with nothing inside me.

I turned on the TV, trying to get some normal life into the
place. I pulled out a chair in the dining room, where I could sit
and watch, but it had dirt and hair like every other surface. I had
to do something productive, and I had a duty towards the animals
– as Claire had reminded me. I crawled under the couch next to
a dead roach on its back to look for Ignats. He wasn't there. The
last dish of yellow squash I'd given him was still in the corner. It

was dried past the mould stage, just a hardened mass. I took the dish to the kitchen, thinking of where he might have gone.

I checked under the bed and in the open closet. I called to him as I headed for the bathroom. "Ignaaats . . . Ignaaats . . ." It felt right to fill that noxious place with the sad whine of my voice.

I saw him as soon as I turned the corner. He was in the bathtub, on the bottom in a few inches of water, legs wide, toes spread, pale, and dead.

I reached in and felt his beaded hide. He was solid. I grabbed him with both hands and raised him, water streaming from his tail running down my arm. In my hurry to get out of the apartment the last time, I had forgotten to drain the tub.

I grabbed the towel off the rack and carried it with me to the dining room table. I sobbed as I walked. I wanted to look at him. Soothe him. I knew somewhere in his reptile brain he must have felt the panic and loneliness of dying in that cold water. I spread the towel with one hand, holding him against my body with the other. I placed him in the middle of the table and stroked from the ridge of spines on his head down the five feet to the end of his tail. A few caps came off of his spines. He was either just starting to shed when he died or it was part of his decomposition.

He was still beautiful. Now I could finally hold him. I took off my shirt and shorts and boosted myself onto the table to lie over him. I knew it was insane, but I wanted to feel his hard scales against my skin, warm him. I pressed my cheek on his short stiff spines and crushed his brittle skin between my breasts. His tail was rigid against my thigh. I thought of how powerful that lashing tail used to be.

I moved forward to feel him hard between my legs. His spines slipped inside of me. I slid myself forward and back to feel the sting. The sharp points raked my false penis and inner tissues with a burning pain, but it was not near the punishment I deserved for this useless sacrifice. I never knew how to love Ig – or anybody. The men flashed before me – Gary, Charlie, Dennis, Enzo. All different connections, all empty in one direction or another, unbalanced. I wasn't the woman for them. I wasn't the woman for anybody. I stayed on my beloved Ig, tight in every muscle, with the cold edge of him between my legs. I choked on my tears and flowing mucus. Surges of nausea swept through me. When my strength was gone, I went limp over him and wept for a long time.

I woke up on the table, sweaty and drooling beside him, with his hard blue-green face resting in the hand against my cheek. It was dusk. I felt the presence of his cage, empty in my peripheral vision, low sun slanting through. Such a solid construction, galvanized wire over a heavy wood skeleton, inescapable – the way I built myself.

I heard music – the TV I'd left on, a talk show. I lifted my head. I was still groggy, weak with grief – and fear of loneliness. A woman was telling her story. She was obsessed with a man who beat her. My eyes moved to the screen. Passion pulled her face taut. She said he'd broken a rib this time, close to her heart. But he wanted her to stay, and she would. Was it love? I knew it was – the worst kind.